THE GAT

BAN
THE GATE

Text Copyright © 2014 Wendy Knight
Illustration Copyright © 2014 Mikey Brooks
Cover design by Mikey Brooks/Lost Treasure Illustrating

Published by: *Six Gate Publishing*.

SIX GATE PUBLISHING

Summary: Thirteen-year-old half-breed banshee, Seven, likes her life. She leads souls safely to Death and she has the planet's most awesome dad and little brother. But a cryptic message from Atlantis asking for her help changes all that. And then there's Death, who has decided it's time to take her brother's soul. Now she's racing across the world, trying to stay one step ahead of Death.

Unfortunately, getting to Atlantis from Ireland isn't easy, and there are evil minions determined to keep her away every time she turns around. But fighting for their lives teaches Seven one very important lesson—she isn't human, and she isn't a banshee. She has to be both if she wants to save her brother and make it back home alive..

Paperback Edition:
ISBN-10: 1939993385
ISBN-13: 978-1-939993-38-0

THE GATES OF ATLANTIS

BANSHEE AT THE GATE
BY: WENDY KNIGHT

GUARDIANS OF THE GATES
BY: LAURA D. BASTIAN

SECRETS OF THE MINE
BY: JULI CALDWELL

MAGICIANS OF THE DEEP
BY: JACLYN WEIST

MADNESS BEHIND THE THRONE
BY: J.R. SIMMONS

BATTLE FOR ACROPOLIS
BY: MIKEY BROOKS

DEDICATION

To my Atlantis team.
None of this would have been possible without you!

MAP OF THE GREAT CITY OF
ATLANTIS

ATLANTIC OCEAN

THE GATES TO ATLANTIS AND THEIR LOCATIONS:

- ALGERIAN MEGALITHS
- ZIMBABWE MINES
- WHARIN BASIN
- DEVILS TRIANGLE
- LOYALTY ISLAND
- HAWAIIAN VOLCANOES
- EASTER ISLAND
- RIO DE JANEIRO
- BERMUDA TRIANGLE
- INDUS RIVER, PAKISTAN

THE GATES OF
ATLANTIS
BANSHEE AT THE GATE

WENDY KNIGHT

CHAPTER ONE:
BIG SISTER BANSHEE

Being a banshee is hard. Being a hybrid banshee who is mostly human is harder.

Seven was used to seeing Death. Only banshees could see him, and Seven handed him souls on a regular basis. Even so, knowing he was coming, that someone was about to die—it made her nervous. So when she saw him standing by the school bus, watching silently, her heart sank a little.

She stopped outside his field of vision, wondering who he watched. His black cloak hid him entirely. She wasn't sure he even had feet, and when he moved, he sort of floated. No, the only part of Death she could see besides his thin white hands were his glowing red eyes. He wasn't a bad guy at all, but his eyes? They were terrifying. A little bit.

Haran was waiting for her, she knew. He was ten and still young enough that it was cool to sit with his big sister, and she loved him enough that she was okay with that. She saw him, bouncing on his toes, looking anxiously for her. Giving up on Death, she hurried to her brother.

"Hey, kiddo. How was school?" she asked, adjusting her bag over her shoulder.

"Good. I got a 100% on my mythology test today." Haran grinned as he fell into step beside her, dark brown eyes sparkling as his brown hair flopped over his eyebrow. He needed a haircut. These were things mothers were good for. Neither of them had a mother, so sometimes haircuts got forgotten. Their dad did the best he could, though, and he did it amazingly well. In Seven's opinion, he was probably the best dad ever.

Seven snorted. "No surprise there." Her brother was absolutely obsessed with mythology. Maybe it came from having a mythological half-sister. She glanced back at Death, wondering if he'd found his target yet, but he was gone. Apparently he wasn't in much of a hurry.

She listened to Haran chatter the entire way home. He knew more about mythology than Seven did, and it was his favorite thing to talk about. They got off the bus as he was explaining naiads, and made it into the house as he started on shape-shifting dragons, which, according to Haran's research, existed. Who knew?

"Hi, Dad!" Seven yelled, dropping her bag on the floor underneath the hook her dad had put there specifically to hold their bags. Haran raced into the kitchen, bag bouncing behind him.

"Hey, Sev. I'm in here. How was school?" Dad called from his office. He worked from home, a single, full-time dad and some sort of computer genius. He'd explained what he did several times, but Seven had never understood it. She'd learned to just smile and nod.

"Good." *Don't ask about my math test. Don't ask about my math test.*

"How was your math test?" he asked as he came around the corner. He looked pointedly at her bag on the floor and raised an eyebrow.

With an exaggerated sigh, she hung her bag on his special hook. "It was . . . I don't think I failed." She winced, peeking at him from her scrunched up eyes.

"You don't think you failed."

"Nope," she said brightly.

"Seven."

"Being thirteen is hard, Dad!"

"Seven."

Her head dropped in defeat and she cursed.

"Language, Seven. We'll get through this. It might mean getting a tutor, though."

He wasn't mad. Of course he wasn't mad. Her dad didn't get mad. Best. Dad. Ever. "I'm open to that. Or a brain transplant might work."

Dad rolled his eyes and tossed a throw pillow at her. She danced out of the way, laughing. He disappeared into the kitchen after Haran, and she could just hear Haran telling him about his test as they both searched for something that might hold Haran's hunger at bay. That boy was constantly eating. Seven's dad said he was going through a growth spurt and if she wasn't careful, Haran would pass her up. She was small for her age, and Haran was perfectly average, and growing like a weed.

She raised her voice so they could hear her as she dug her math book out of her bag. "I'm going to check on Atlantis. You've got dinner tonight, right?"

"I'm on it!" Dad yelled back. She heard the clatter of pots and pans, and then cursing.

She grinned as she sprinted up the stairs, taking them two at a time. "Language, Dad!" He may or may not have been bellowing by the time she shut her door.

She didn't have any friends in Atlantis, but she kept hoping. Seven was supposed to have mystical powers, which would have been cool—except she didn't know how to use them. Banshees were supposedly all terrifying and stuff, but no one knew she was a banshee. No one was really scared of her except other magical creatures and animals. Also, she was the only one who could see Death when he came to visit.

She settled on her bed and picked up her tablet. It had a pretty black and red case that matched the rest of her room. Dad said she wasn't allowed to take it to school, so it sat on her desk all day, alone and pathetic. "Hi little one." Since animals were afraid of her, she'd never had a pet. Electronics had taken their place in her heart.

The tablet blinked to life and she toed off her shoes and wrapped her blankets around her like a nest. She tapped on the internet and navigated her way to SplashSpace—a social media network for all creatures magical. It was based in Atlantis, but anyone with magic in their blood could access it, using the same technology that opened the gates going into the city, apparently. She'd never been. Nor had she any desire to ever leave Ireland or the families she protected.

She didn't have much to do with Atlantis. Most magical creatures avoided her. Banshees were sorely misunderstood, in her opinion. Although her mother, the mighty Six, had been to Atlantis once and had done some major damage . . . giving the Atlantian community the wrong impression.

But…

But there had been rumors. Things her dad had heard, probably from her mother. Seven did not speak to Six. Ever. But her dad still did, from time to time. When Six's families crossed paths with his village. Anyway, the rumors. Things were changing in Atlantis. If things changed in Atlantis, they affected the whole magical world. So Seven had been keeping closer tabs on SplashSpace lately, looking for truth to the rumors—that some guy named Phoibos was trying to close the gates, and that all magic would die off. She'd never met this Phoibos guy, but she knew already that she didn't like him even a little.

On her homepage, she had one new message. She never got messages. One of the thrills of being a banshee—they were a harbinger of death. Everyone was afraid to talk to them on the off chance that one might say, "Hey, by the way— you're gonna die today."

"As if that's how it works," Seven muttered as she dragged her finger over the message icon and tapped it. No, no, one did not simply see a person and know they would die. One saw a person and saw Death following them. It was way creepier than most magical creatures understood. And only the banshee could do it.

"Are you the banshee Seven?"

Seven's eyebrows shot up. She scanned the page, studying the other person's profile. *Alat* was the username, with a scorpion avatar. She wasn't sure what to do with that information. Biting her lip, she finally wrote back, *"Why do you ask that?"*

The answer came immediately. Apparently, *Alat* was online. *"Your username kinda gave you away."*

Seven threw herself back on her pillows, disrupting her nest. "Right. I'm such an idiot." In her defense, it wasn't everyday she had a conversation with something else magical. She sat up and answered. *"Oh. Right. I knew I was being too obvious. Do I know you?"*

"Probably not. I'm from Atlantis. I wanted to ask you a favor."

"Of course you do," Seven sighed. No one wanted to be friends with the banshee. She tapped her nail against her teeth for several seconds, trying to formulate a polite response. Her dad drilled into her head—is it nice? Is it kind? Is it necessary? No? Then don't say it. He may have ruined her for confrontation. *"What's up?"*

Yes, that would work.

"I sent you a private message about something that's been going on here. Did you see it?"

A private message? Isn't that what it was? *"No. Give me a second."* Frowning, she scanned her profile again. "Oh. Duh." There it was, that little blinking thingie. Before she could figure out how to open the blinking thingie, *Alat* was typing again.

"We really need to get the word out that the gates are being messed with and that we can't let that happen. We want to have the magic people up top throw a fit and make the Ruling Counsel do something about the gates. They have to make sure no more get closed and that they do something about reopening the ones that are shut down."

Ah. This was what she'd been hearing rumors about. They were shutting the gates. She ignored the instant message for a second so she could read the direct message. Several of the gates, apparently, were already closed. If all the gates closed, magic would die everywhere. Or at least, that was the rumor.

But it had nothing to do with her. She lived in Ireland. She was only a hybrid. She had no magical friends. And if magic died, she'd become human. She'd grow up, have kids, and die. It wasn't such a bad life. Even if she wanted to help, what could she do? Her families needed her here. She had souls to take. Deaths to forewarn. *"I'm sorry,"* she wrote back. *"I can't really help you."*

"Sure you can. You could come here and bring any other magic people with you to help us with our cause. If we get enough down here, the Ruling Council will have to take us seriously."

Seven snorted. Yeah, because everyone takes a banshee seriously. Mostly, they run screaming. Which was a little bit ironic. *"I'm sorry. I really am. I can't come to Atlantis. I have responsibilities up here. My families need me. I can't leave them."*

Alat tried again. *"Could you at least think about it?"*

Seven sighed. She didn't want to be mean. *"I can pass the word to any magical creature I see, but I don't see many. They . . . seem to be afraid of me. I'm sorry I can't come myself."*

Guilt gnawed at her. She should help. But her families. They needed her. *Alat* wrote back, "*I understand. I would really appreciate the help in spreading the word though. Could you send a message to your mom and all your contacts I might not know? And have them friend me if they want more information?*"

Yeah, that she could do. Her whole . . . she checked her friend list . . . Nineteen contacts. Half of them were friends of her mother's. Six wasn't a hybrid anymore, like Seven. She lacked a physical body—she'd given it up when she left her humanity behind to become a full banshee. Without a physical body, she had no physical strength. Thus, Six wasn't as powerful as Seven, and less scary. Her mother's friends took pity on her. *"Of course,"* Seven sent. *"I think it's so awesome that you are doing this to make sure things don't go wrong. I know it's important to keep the gates open. I wish I could help more. But I'll do what I can."*

"*Thanks so much,*" Alat wrote back.

Seven buried herself in her blankets. This had been exhausting. Homework was so much less stressful. "*I've got to go. Good luck.*" Before anything else could catch her, she left SplashSpace and shut off her tablet. Then she stuffed it under her pillow to be safe.

She leaned over the side of her bed and stretched for her homework, just out of reach. With a screech, she toppled from her makeshift nest and landed in a heap on the floor, her math book jutting painfully into her ribs. Her dad's feet pounded up the stairs and her door burst open— or what was left of it.

"You broke the door," Dad said needlessly.

Seven blushed, trying to untangle herself from the blankets. "It was an accident. I fell."

He sighed, rubbing his hands over his face. "Being a banshee and all," he looked at her pointedly, "how about we learn to not scream every time we fall or trip, 'kay?"

"Good idea, Dad. I'll work on it."

Dad grinned. "Thanks."

Haran shouted from the bottom of the stairs, "Is she alive?"

Dad glanced over his shoulder and then looked back at Seven. "You okay, by the way?"

She raised an eyebrow, finally shoving the rest of the mess off with her feet. "Yeah. I'll survive."

Her dad stuck his head out of the broken door. "She's alive!" he yelled.

Seven rolled her eyes. "Could you hand me the pencil on my desk? Don't wanna risk tripping on my way over and blowing a hole through the outer wall. Winter's coming, you know."

He reached for the pencil, dangling it just out of reach of her outstretched hand. "You're using your magical abilities as an excuse for laziness. Not cool, Seven. Not cool."

She grinned and snatched the pencil. "Just keeping you on your toes, Dad."

CHAPTER TWO:
DEATH DOESN'T
HAVE FEET

Haran waited for Seven on the school steps. "Hey kiddo," she said as she walked through the double doors, trying unsuccessfully to get her backpack straps on without twisting them.

"Hey, big sis. You're slow today."

Seven nodded, sighing. "This day, it is not my friend. Long and boring. Ready?" Haran nodded as he pulled his bag over his shoulder with no problem and rose to his feet. "What's wrong? Did someone surprise you, and you blew up the gym?"

She quirked her lips at him, scowling. "No. I didn't . . . math isn't fun."

"Ah." Haran nodded wisely, like he wasn't

ten years old. "You got your math test back."

She nodded, dropping her head to her chest. "I'm gonna be a full banshee one day. I won't even know what math is. Why do I have to go to school?"

Haran dodged around some bigger kids and came back to her side, brushing his floppy hair out of his eyes. "Well, for one, I think Dad hopes you'll choose the human path instead, in which case . . . he somehow thinks math will still be useful. I haven't figured that one out yet."

Seven chuckled, nodding.

"Or two, you know . . . maybe banshees do have to know math. Like, maybe you have to know the amount of souls you're guarding, divided by the number of souls you've handed to Death, multiplied by the amount of souls you missed—" She frowned at him and he ducked his head and hurried on. "—as if you'd miss any, right? And then find the square root of it all. I think that's a total possibility in the banshee world."

Seven smiled and rolled her eyes. "Right. Makes complete sense." In reality, Seven felt every single soul she'd ever handed over to Death. Each one had a special place in her heart, like the loss of a very dear friend. She wouldn't need math to remember them, even after centuries of being a banshee.

Haran laughed, because he was Haran and he was always happy and always laughing. He balanced Seven's sadness, since she was constantly mourning the loss of her souls.

As if the very thought conjured him, Death suddenly appeared across the parking lot. He was so out of place amid the giggling, screaming, playing children. He floated just off the ground, robes billowing around him, so she *still* couldn't tell if he had feet. His hands were clasped in front of him, mostly hidden. The only thing she could see clearly were his eyes. They glowed beneath the folds of his hood, and Seven's heart stopped.

Death was staring right at her brother.

"No. No, no no no. You can't have him," she moaned. "Haran, come on. Hurry." She grabbed his hand and dragged him onto the bus. Death didn't follow, which meant they had time. How much, Seven didn't know.

"What's wrong with you? You look like there's a monster outside your window," Haran asked as they settled into their seats. "Wait, *is* there a monster outside your window?" He craned his neck, trying to see around her. She forced a shaky laugh but refused to look away from Death, lest he move. If he wanted her brother, there wasn't much she could do to prevent it. But that didn't mean she wouldn't try.

She sank next to him, leaning her cheek against the top of his head. "Nothing's wrong, little brother. It will be okay."

Mythology had painted Seven's kind as scary and evil and deadly. But mythology was wrong. Banshees were more like comforters. They cried and mourned the loss of life, protected the Celtic families they were loyal to, and when the time came, they held the dying's hand and walked with them into the afterlife, passing them safely off to Death.

Not the most fun job ever.

Seven loved it, though. She loved the peace she could bring. She loved that she could comfort in a terrifying time. One day, she would have to choose—be a full banshee, or a full human. She was the seventh hybrid banshee ever. And no one had ever chosen to become human.

But when Death had come to summon her brother? Suddenly she wasn't so fond of being a banshee. At all.

"Dad? Dad! I need to talk to you!" Seven dropped her bag by the door, under the hook. Haran copied her before running off to the kitchen for the afterschool snack Dad had waiting, just like every day before. Just like he wasn't about to die.

Their dad made amazing chocolate chip cookies. Also, he raised a hybrid banshee without batting an eye, despite the fact that he was human. Before he'd fallen in love with a banshee on a "banshee break", he'd had no clue that mythological creatures even existed. He deserved a medal. She would give him one, if he'd answer her already.

"What's up, Seven?" he asked, poking his head out of his office. Ah. He was working. Right. She hurried in, shutting the door behind her.

"We have a problem. We need to leave. Pack everything up and let's go."

He raised an eyebrow and hid a smirk, but she could still see it, hiding there behind his solemn expression. "Bad day at school?"

She crossed her arms over her chest, biting her lip. "Dad, Death is here. And he's waiting for Haran."

He sat back with a whoosh, like the time when Haran had accidentally thrown a bowling ball and hit him in the stomach. "Are you sure?" His voice shook, just a little.

Seven nodded, feeling tears snaking their way down her cheek as she sank into the chair across from him.

"How long?" he asked.

"I don't know. But we can outrun him! We can—"

Her dad leaned forward, his elbows on his knees. "Can you call your mother?"

Seven swallowed hard. Her mother, the mighty Six. No human feelings or emotions at all. She was like a super banshee. Seven was pretty sure she didn't remember she had a daughter. But she did remember Seven's dad. Her one human attachment.

"Why?" she whispered. Dad couldn't really want Seven's mother to take her little brother, could he? Was he just giving up? Seven opened her mouth to set him straight, but he spoke first.

"She might know something you don't. She might know how to stop Death."

Hope bloomed in her chest, and Seven nodded. Yes, her mother would know. She would ask her. She would sing, and Six would come because that was the way of the banshee. "Whatcha doin?" Haran asked, popping in. Seven whirled, searching behind him, watching for Death. But Death was not there.

"That's a good sign," she muttered aloud.

Haran raised an eyebrow at her. "I think Seven needs an early bedtime. She's been weird all day."

Seven forced a laugh and Dad chuckled, standing up to ruffle Haran's brown floppy hair, the exact shade as his own. In fact, Haran looked like a miniature version of their dad. Seven, not so much. Banshees had bright red hair. Pale skin.

Green eyes. Six was beautiful. Seven hoped one day she would be as pretty as her mother, except maybe with a physical body because Six was a ghost. And Seven wasn't. Not yet, anyway.

Dad was American. He'd met Six while on vacation and had stayed in Ireland to raise Seven because her soul belonged to the Celtic families she protected. As previously mentioned, Best. Dad. Ever.

"I've gotta do . . . some stuff . . . " She bounced out of her chair, squeezing Haran's hand as she passed him. "I'll see you guys at dinner."

"Where are you going?" Haran followed her out of her dad's office.

"Nowhere, Haran. Don't you have homework?" she asked as he stayed right on her heels. She finally paused at the door. She couldn't very well have a conversation about saving his life with her banshee mother while he stood right next to her.

"Nope." He smiled innocently. Too innocently. She wasn't going to get rid of him easily.

"Haran, I need some privacy. It's girl stuff.

Go play." She put her hand on the doorknob, but he only rocked back on his heels, scowling at her.

"Girl stuff doesn't happen *outside*, Seven."

"Haran!" she swung the door open, turning away from him. "Go do some—" Her words died in her throat. Standing on their front stoop was something so awful even Seven's nightmares could never have come up with it. Vaguely the shape of a dog, but bigger than a man. Matted, shaggy fur, spikes along its back, and from its jaws dripped sparks and flames. And horns curled out of its head.

Seven screamed. The dog stumbled backward under the force and she slammed the door. "Run. *Run*, Haran!" She grabbed his shoulders and spun him, pushing him hard. He sprinted up the stairs. "Dad! Call the—" Seven's terrified brain couldn't even think who he should call. The police? Animal control? Their dad came out of his office, staring at her in surprise, and she grabbed his hand and tugged as she raced past.

They flew up the stairs. Seven slammed the door behind her and locked it, then ran to her dad's room after Haran. Her dad followed her, still completely baffled. "What's going on?" he yelled, because Seven and Haran were both shrieking and running through the room like demented, headless chickens.

"There's this dog thing—" Haran started. Seven cut him off,

"It was a demon—"

"But it looked like a dog—"

"It was a dog demon! With fire in its mouth!" she squealed.

Haran nodded vigorously. "And Seven screamed and knocked it backward—"

"I didn't mean to! It scared me!" Seven objected.

The door burst into flames.

Her dad joined their shrieking, shoving them both toward the French doors. He had a lovely wrap-around balcony with adorable curving stairs leading to the garden. He wrenched the doors open and shoved them through. Seven immediately sprinted to the stairs, taking them two at a time and leaping past the last several. She could hear Haran and her dad right behind her, but when she risked a glance over her shoulder, the dog demon thing burst through the French doors, shattering glass all around it. It leaped from the balcony, landing directly in front of them.

Seven screamed. The dog stumbled back and Seven wished that she knew how to be the big, powerful hybrid banshee her mother had been rumored to be before she'd given it up. It snarled as she stumbled backward, tripping over Haran. "Run, Haran," she whispered, but he didn't run. Her little brother, the one who Death was already waiting for, stepped in front of her. To protect her.

The dog thing snarled and snapped and they all jumped like they were connected by wires or something. Her dad had a grip like steel on both of their arms, dragging them backward. They stumbled over their own feet and each others' feet and anything else in their way that could possibly slow their progress any more.

The dog demon paced with them, a wicked smile on its horrid face, like it was enjoying their terror. But it had had enough. With a low growl, it leaped forward.

They were going to die.

But it was yanked right out of the air by something bigger, something darker. Like a man but with the substance of a shadow, but it could hold the demon and Seven's mind couldn't make it make sense. In front of her wide, terror-frozen eyes, it tore the demon dog to shreds with long, black claws. And then it looked at her.

It had eyes. They were red and glowing—demon eyes. But the rest of it was just . . . just a shadow, but not a shadow, she could see now. Like a giant, if a shadow had swallowed a giant. All black, but definitely solid. "Please. Please don't hurt us," Seven whimpered.

Her dad pushed them both behind him. "Get away from them!"

"I'm here to protect the banshee, idiot human." Its voice didn't sound entirely solid. In fact, it reminded Seven of when she heard her mother speak—like more wind than voice.

And, perhaps more importantly, "You're—you're here to protect me? Why?" Seven peeked around her dad's shoulder at the shadow creature.

"She's not a banshee. She's a hybrid." Haran

peeked around the other shoulder, and Seven wanted to strangle him. "See, real banshees usher the dead into the next life. They cry—which is the wailing everyone's always talking about. But they don't have a body. They don't have physical powers. They can scream, but they couldn't knock a dog the size of a horse back like Seven did on accident." Haran grinned at her proudly. Why was he not terrified, as she was? "Hybrid banshees can call an army of dead to do their bidding and their scream can kill things. And their eyes can shoot fire. Or at least, that's what I've heard."

"You've heard? She hasn't done any of these things?" It looked at Seven, "You haven't done any of these things?" The shadow thing raised a shadow-eyebrow, as if it was perfectly logical for Seven to go skipping into the back yard and light the forest on fire with her eyes while screaming for her army of undead to come play tag.

"No. I've never needed to. Banshees aren't scary. We're . . . broken-hearted. Loyal. Protective. I'm a peaceful hybrid banshee," she whispered.

"She could if she needed to," Haran said, perfectly confident in his frozen-in-fear sister.

The shadow thing scoffed. "I believe, human-child, that if ever she would have needed to, now would have been it." He looked pointedly at Seven and she felt a blush rise from her toes to her hairline. She was weak. Banshees weren't supposed to be strong. They weren't warriors!

"Why are you protecting her? And how do we know we can trust you?" her dad asked.

"You don't know. But you don't have a choice. I'm here to escort her to Atlantis."

Seven's heart stopped. "Atlantis? I can't go to Atlantis. My—" *brother* "—souls need me here. I have to be here so they don't die alone." She swallowed what felt like a boulder lodged in her throat. She had to escort Haran home. His final home.

"You do not have a choice. Come, little banshee." He reached for her, plucking her easily from behind her father, his arm bending through the shadows, hiding from light. She squealed, twisting and kicking, and his arm shimmered. He promptly dropped her, his eyes glowing more evilly red than before.

Seven crossed her arms over her chest, mostly to hide the trembling. She was not made for confrontation. "Why do we need to go to Atlantis? Why can't you protect me here?"

The creature's red eyes narrowed dangerously. "We cannot stay here because you have to go to Atlantis to defeat Lady Kraken."

"Me. Defeat—defeat Lady Kraken?" Seven stuttered. "I can't even defeat my math homework."

"The seer saw it. She sent us to protect you. We're to bring you to the gate to kill Lady Kraken."

Seven turned her head just enough that she could speak to Haran and keep one wary eye on the shadow guy. "What's a kraken?"

"Big. Lots of legs. Very strong. Didn't know they were *girls* though."

Oh dear.

"I think your seer saw wrong. Maybe a different magical creature with similar red hair. It happens all the time." Seven nodded encouragingly.

"The seer saw *his* death, too. But you already knew that, didn't you?" The creature pointed one long claw over her shoulder, at Haran. Seven swallowed hard, raising wide, panicked eyes to her father.

"Saw my death? You know—Am I going to die?" Haran asked, scrabbling backward away from them all.

Seven deliberately turned her back on the creature, holding her hands out, trying to placate her little brother. "Haran, I knew, but I didn't know how. Death hasn't told me yet. We were trying to figure out a way to save you when the dog thing showed up."

"Gwygii."

"What?" Seven asked, confused, heartsick, scared.

"The creature was a gwygii. No doubt sent by Lady Kraken." Shadow-thing sounded bored.

"Can we get back to the fact that I'm going to *die?*" Haran yelled, hands on his hips, but Seven could see past the bravado to the scared little boy.

"You aren't going to die. I won't—I won't let

29

him take you."

"You're a banshee, Seven, not Death. You can't stop him. I know my mythology." His little voice cracked and Seven's heart broke. "So," Haran swung away from her, toward the shadow. "Tell me about my death. What did your seer see?"

"She saw that if the banshee brought you to drink from the Fountain of Youth, you would not die."

Seven had formed an argument. She had it all planned out in her head, and she was mustering her courage to actually say it. But the shadow guy's words stopped her short. "I can save him?" she whispered.

He nodded once. "Yes."

Seven turned, slowly, so slowly, as if the entire world was trying to crush her through the floor. She met her dad's eyes; they were full of tears. For several seconds, they had a silent conversation, but Seven knew his answer by the sad set of his shoulders. "I'll go," she whispered.

The shadow leaned back, almost amused. "It isn't like you had a choice, little banshee."

"If I'm supposed to defeat a kraken, then I think I could figure out how to fight you off if I needed to," Seven snapped, still watching her father. He'd been such a good father. So supportive. So strong. He'd always known one day she would leave him—they both had. But they always thought it would be because she'd become a full banshee. Not because she was running off to face her death. But this—this was the right thing to do. Haran needed her. And so did Atlantis.

The shadow was growling at her, but she cut him off, surprised at her own boldness. "I'll go with you if I can bring them *and* you can promise me their safety." She motioned to Haran and her father with her head.

"They are human. They will not survive the journey."

"Then I won't go." At the shadow thing's outraged glare, she paced forward. "You're the one who told me the seer saw my brother being saved at the Fountain of Youth. You told me that for a reason."

She wanted to glare at him until he agreed.

She tried, but instead she flushed bright red and had to look away. She was not a confrontational person. At all.

"Fine. You may take the boy, but not your father. His age will slow us down. End of discussion. Get your things," he finally snarled. Seven nearly squealed. She'd won. She didn't think she'd win, but she had.

And then she realized what he'd said. It was time to go. She had to leave her father. Her families. She'd never been gone away from him or them for even one night. Her souls might die before she could make it back to escort them to heaven. She covered her face and sobbed, running to her father's open arms.

CHAPTER THREE:
DON'T PET THE GIANT, FLAMING DEMON DOGS

D o you have your tablet? Your phone? Charger? Make sure you've got something to keep me updated with."

"Yep. Got them all." Oh, her tablet. SplashSpace. Seven thunked herself onto the floor next to her bag and dug her tablet out, turning it on and waiting impatiently. Haran thundered down the stairs, dropping his bags near hers by the door. "Almost ready," Seven said without glancing up. She couldn't. Couldn't watch Haran say goodbye to their dad. Couldn't think about the fact that she would have to, too. Instead she shut it all out and logged on to

SplashSpace. She found her messages and hurriedly typed one back to *Alat*. *"I'm on my way."*

Then she tucked her tablet into her bag and stood up. Haran was crying. He tried to be brave—he always tried to be brave. He brushed at his tears with his sleeve and turned away so she couldn't see. Her dad was crying, too, and by the time Seven took the three steps across the hallway to his side, she was crying, as well. "I don't—I don't know how to say goodbye." She looked up into his face, so kind. Always. So kind, so patient. "You're the best dad ever. I would never leave if I didn't—if I didn't have to."

He smoothed her hair away from her face as one single tear slid down his cheek. "I know. But I knew this day would come. My little banshee girl would have to leave me to save the day." He nodded, as if agreeing with himself. "Just come back to me, okay?" He looked up at Haran. "Both of you, come back."

"I will. I promise." She hugged him tight and the little girl in her wanted to scream and kick and never leave. But the banshee in her let go and stepped back. "I love you, Dad. Be safe while we're gone."

Something grabbed her by the back of her shirt and ripped her out of the doorway.

"Dad!" she screeched, reaching even though she'd just let him go. Haran grabbed their bags and ran after them, for one second obliterating any view of their dad that Seven had. But then Haran moved and she could see Dad again. He slowly raised one hand in goodbye.

"The gwygii are coming. We have to move or he'll be in danger." The shadow's voice rasped as his claws scraped the back of her neck. Seven squirmed around so she could see where they were going. Waiting at the edge of the village was a whole group of monstrous shadows.

Herd? Flock? What is a group of shadows called? Whatever the name for a bunch of mythical creatures, it was a terrifying sight. Five of them, as far as Seven could tell, all with big, sharp teeth, glowing red eyes, and claws longer than Seven's arm.

Haran had to sprint to keep up, and by the time they reached the end of the road and entered into the trees, he was panting, his cheeks pink.

"Slow down! Or carry him. Your legs are longer than his entire body!"

"No! No no, no need to carry me," Haran yelped between gasps for air. "I'm fine."

"Haran, they aren't going to eat you." Seven wriggled until she was free of her shirt, and fell to the ground. Luckily, she had a tank top on underneath or things could have been very embarrassing. The shadow snorted and reached for her, but she scrabbled backward out of the way. "I can walk."

"You cannot walk. You are too slow."

"Then I'll fly."

"You can't fly. We can't protect you if you fly."

"Oh." She could have come up with a witty retort, given time. But she wasn't given time. A gwygii, at least as big as the one that attacked the day before, burst straight out of the ground in front of them. Seven screamed and dove backward, accidentally tackling Haran. They both crashed to the ground but the dog thing…

The dog thing shot backward.

The force of Seven's surprise was so much

that her scream moved the entire gigantic beast backward several yards. Three of the shadows attacked, and the other two snatched Haran and Seven up off the ground and ran.

"I thought we agreed we could run?" Seven asked as they bounced along with the hurtling shadow.

"We did not agree. And there is a whole pack of gwygii coming. Your scream might throw one back on its haunches, but it will not stop them all. We must get to the Loch."

Haran looked at her with wide, frightened eyes in his pale face, but he didn't say a word. They ran in silence for several minutes, so fast the trees blurred and the wind tugged and pulled at her hair. She had just started thinking that maybe the gwygii had given up when the howls started.

She'd heard howling before. There were wolves in the forests outside the village, although they'd never bothered anyone. Dogs bayed every time sirens sounded. But this—this was not like anything she'd ever experienced. It made her blood run beyond cold to absolutely frozen, so that it felt like she might crack and break. "Cover your ears!" she yelled to Haran, but he was three steps ahead of her and already had his ears covered, his eyes squinched tight, and had curled himself into a ball around the shadowy hand carrying him. If they survived this, her little brother was going to have nightmares for life.

The shadow lengthened his stride and they bounded through the forest. Others joined around them, in front, behind, and on each side, forming a protective barrier. Seven scrabbled like a monkey up the shadow's arm so she could see behind them, and immediately wished she hadn't. When shadow man had said the whole pack of gwygii was coming, he hadn't exaggerated. There were ten, fifteen, maybe more. As she watched, one leaped forward, catching the shadow directly behind them. He fell, screaming, under their attack.

"You know those special powers you're supposed to have?" Haran yelled, finally finding his voice through the terror. "They'd be handy right now, Sev!"

Seven blinked at him. She *was* supposed to have powers. She could scream and maybe slow them down. Or . . . laser from her eyes? She wasn't even sure how to do that. She'd accidentally shrieked and knocked things down before, but she'd never accidentally fried someone by blinking wrong. And . . . army of the dead? She thought about that one. She could feel them, sometimes. The lost souls who hadn't had a banshee to hand them safely over to Death. But she couldn't see them. She'd never had a conversation with one, or asked them to join her army in case she was ever chased by demons.

Screaming it was.

She twisted so she wasn't all tangled like a pretzel and took a deep breath. She screamed, terrified, high-pitched, too human. The dog-faces of the gwygii flamed as if in pain, and the first few stumbled. But they barely slowed before they were leaping and snarling and spitting fire again.

"Come on, Seven! Six could do better than that and she doesn't even have a physical body!"

Oh yes. Compare her to her mother. "That was a low blow, Haran," she muttered. She'd never seen Six use her powers for anything, but she'd heard rumors. Rumors that she'd gone ballistic in Atlantis and screamed at everything around her. She'd caused a lot of damage but she hadn't killed anyone.

Another gwygii leaped and caught the shadow guy's heel. He stumbled, pitching her forward across the forest floor, as three more dog demons landed on top of him.

He'd saved her.

He'd saved her brother.

She scrambled to her knees and shoved herself to her feet. She dug way down deep and shoved her human half aside, searching, searching. There it was. The banshee half she hardly ever used because becoming a banshee meant she left a bit of her human self behind every time. With some mental sort of fist, she grabbed that banshee half and clung to it.

And then she screamed again.

This time, the entire forest shook. The shadow creatures around her stumbled and fell. The trees quaked and leaves scattered and swirled like a mini tornado. The gwygii pack skidded to a halt, some of them trying to backpedal, which in any other time would have been hilarious—it wasn't every day you saw a demon dog trying to run backward.

But it was not hilarious. It was terrifying. She was screaming with everything she had and they were only stumbling around like they were in a powerful wind—

The one closest to her exploded.

He'd been on top of her shadow creature guy. Then the other two burst into flames, their ashes shooting backward, igniting the other dogs. The entire pack combusted, their howls echoing through Seven's skull, her blood, her heart. And then there was nothing but the sound of crackling flames as their fire went out.

"Should we call the fire department or shoot them with a fire extinguisher or something?" Haran asked, his voice muffled from being half-buried under the shadow creature carrying him.

Seven turned to stare at him, feeling as if she was coming back to herself from a very long distance. Her brother. *Her brother.* Her human brother. She was human. "Haran! Are you okay?" She snapped back together and raced toward him, tugging him free.

"Yeah. I'm fine. Is he dead? Are they all dead?" Haran prodded his shadow guy with his foot, looking at Seven in alarm when he didn't move.

She hurried over to the one that had saved her, kneeling next to him. It was hard to tell if there were injuries. Sort of like light shining through torn spots. Had she killed them all? She hadn't thought about them, only the dog demons. But then again, she had no idea what she was doing. "Haran? I think I killed the shadow guys!"

The thing at her feet groaned, slowly sitting up. Around her, the others pushed themselves to their feet, some swaying like the ground still shook. "Oh thank goodness," Seven breathed.

"We are not shadow guys." Her creature glared, red eyes narrowed. "We are Egyptian guardian demons."

Seven's jaw dropped and she looked at Haran, who inched closer to her. "Say what now?"

"We're guardian demons. Not all demons are evil, you know. Just like not all banshees are dangerous. I am Akhenaton."

Haran, ever the one to speak his mind, didn't hesitate. "All demons aren't evil? Are you sure?"

"There's no way I can pronounce your name," Seven said, trying to ease the sting of Haran's statement.

He ignored her, staring at Haran with distaste. "No, all demons are not evil. And you, human, are of no use to us. You are only here because of her. Do not forget that."

Seven stepped between them and intercepted his glare. "He's just a kid. He doesn't know better. What is a guardian demon? And . . . do you happen to have a nickname?"

Akhenaton scoffed. It was weird, such a human sound coming from a giant shadow. "I do not have a nickname."

Another of the guardian demons approached them. "Another pack of gwygii arises. We must move or we will never make it."

"My sister can take care of them," Haran boasted. Seven couldn't help but smile at the pride in his voice, even as she shook her head.

"That was hard. I'm not sure I can do it again."

Akhenaton looked at her, the red eyes dimming just a bit so he looked sadder, and less terrifying. "You had best learn quickly, little banshee. Lady Kraken will not give up just because you ask nicely."

He picked her up, and another guardian demon picked Haran up, and they were loping through the forest again before she had time to object. If she knew how to fly, she'd be able to fly faster than they could run—or so the rumors said. But she could not fly. She didn't know how to have laser eyes. She hadn't a clue how to summon the dead.

But she was a banshee. And she could scream.

CHAPTER FOUR:
THE LOCH NESS MONSTER
IS PURPLE. WHO KNEW?

Seven wasn't sure how long they ran. She dozed off and on. It was a weightless sort of feeling, being carried by a shadow creature. She knew they moved super fast as they flitted through the forest, like faster than her dad's car on a nicely paved road. And as the sun set, they were even quicker, fading into one spreading shadow and reappearing in another a hundred feet ahead—in just seconds.

"Where are we going?" she asked Akhenaton when the moon had risen high above them. "By the way, I'm going to call you Akie."

"We're going to the Loch Ness. We should be there within the hour and—" he stopped, stumbled over his own feet. "—what? You're going to call me what?"

"I can't pronounce your name," she said in a small voice. The voice she used on her dad when he was resistant to one of her brilliant schemes. Ideas. Brilliant *ideas*. She made her green eyes as big and round as they would go and she stared up at him, jutting her lip.

He caved and she inwardly squealed with triumph. "That is the most ridiculous name I've ever been forced to hear. But fine. If that is what you can pronounce . . . "

She grinned.

And the howls started.

Her blood ran cold, just as it had the first time she'd heard them. The gwygii had found them. They were coming.

Akie lengthened his stride, and as one, the rest of the group followed him. They crashed through the forest, diving through shadows, sprinting across patches of light. Seven scrambled up Akie's arm so she could look over his shoulder, feeling distinctly like a baby about to be burped. In the far off distance, but not far enough, she could see the dripping flames from the dog-like mouths. A pack even bigger than the first one. There was no way she could fight them off.

"Why are they doing this? Why are they hunting us?" Seven cried.

Akie tucked her under his arm like a football and she curled up to make herself as small as possible. "They are Phoibos's minions. Lady Kraken must be sending them to stop you."

"Who is Phoibos?" Haran yelled. Did he *not* realize they were running for their very lives right now?

Akie too, apparently, thought having polite conversation was enjoyable during nightly runs through the forest with dog demons chasing them. Because he answered, almost conversationally, "Phoibos is the one ordering the gates closed. He's trying to rid Atlantis of all the hybrids."

Seven felt like he'd slapped her. "All the hybrids? Like me? And you're *taking* me there?"

The red eyes landed on her briefly before jumping back to the forest floor. They'd been running for hours and hours and he wasn't even winded. "Yes. I'm taking you there to stop him."

Seven tilted her head. "I thought I was only supposed to fight Lady Kraken." They really, really needed to focus on surviving right now. She peeked over his shoulder, to see how close the gwygii were. She could hear their howls, but the dogs were just . . . not there.

Akie and the others slowed to their regular loping pace. "That is the beginning. The seer saw you standing with others to stop Phoibos's wrath."

"Great. That's awesome. Where did the dogs go?"

"They're circling around in front of us." The way Akie said it, so calmly, like he'd expected it, made absolutely no sense.

He stopped running and put her down. "You must make it to the loch. Once there, sing with your banshee voice. Help will come."

Haran, too, was on his feet now, looking around them in sheer panic. "You aren't coming with us?" he asked, his voice high-pitched with fright. The howls were coming closer, and

Seven's entire body broke out in goose bumps.

"I don't know how to sing with my banshee voice!" she said, but Akie was fading away. "Why are you leaving us? Where are you going?" She stomped her foot, "You said you would protect me!"

Akie's voice wafted on the breeze toward her. "Nessie does not like demons . . . "

Nessie. As in the Loch Ness monster? Which meant they were in Scotland . . . Seven had lived in Ireland her whole life and somehow they'd passed clear out of it and into Scotland without even having a chance to say goodbye. Something tore in her heart, a little bit. Banshees weren't meant to leave Ireland.

"Seven!" Haran cried and tugged on her arm. She spun, looking the way his horrified gaze had frozen, and screeched.

The gwygiis were coming.

"Nessie guards the tunnel to Egypt. Ask for her permission to allow you to enter."

"Akie! Nessie's in water!" But her Egyptian guardian demon was gone. Seven grabbed Haran's hand and ran, sprinting through the forest, wishing she could do the shadow hop thing Akie had done.

"Seven!" Haran panted, because unlike the shadow creatures, he *did* get tired, "They're coming closer!"

Seven risked a look over her shoulder. It was true, the gwygii were close enough now that she could see the glowing red eyes through the flames drooling from their gaping mouths.

She should never have looked back.

Because while she was looking back, she didn't watch where she was going. She tripped over a root and pitched forward, taking Haran down with her. Before either one could make it to their knees, the dog demons were upon them. This time, when Seven closed her eyes and dug for her banshee half, it wasn't nearly so hard to find. She screamed, screamed in terror and anger and frustration, but mostly terror, and she couldn't even open her eyes because she was afraid they would burst from their sockets.

But she felt the heat, heard the howls of pain and the explosions. "Seven! You can't get them all. Get up! Get up!" Haran was tugging on her arm, trying to pull her to her feet. She opened her eyes to an inferno, but he was right. Beyond the bonfire in front of her, more gwygii were trying to fight their way through. She surged to her feet and spun, racing toward the loch, being careful not to trip over roots or run into trees. That would be a definite death sentence.

She tried to avoid Death as much as possible.

She started screaming before they reached the water. She also prayed that there weren't any humans in the vicinity, because she doubted very much that Nessie would make an appearance if there were people nearby. Rumor had it, she was camera shy. Haran skidded to a stop on the grass, his shoes, tattered and muddy now, just touching the lapping waves. Behind them, the dogs' howls were coming closer. Too fast. Much too fast.

Seven screamed again and again, and with each scream the waves rose higher and higher until she and Haran were both soaked from the spray of the surf. The water rose at least twenty feet above them before it crashed down on them like pouring rain. Seven ducked her head, trying to hide from the deluge.

When the water cleared and she could open her eyes, Nessie stood before her.

Haran, of course, studied the sea monster with open curiosity and absolutely no fear. He probably already knew her exact dimensions and what her favorite color was. But Seven had never seen her and she didn't do a lot of mythological research, so the sight of Nessie scared her.

A lot.

Every picture Seven had ever seen showed the ancient sea monster looking like a brontosaurus. And they weren't wrong, at least from the body up. But instead of legs, she had flippers, and while Seven had always imagined dinosaurs to have scaly skin, Nessie's was smooth, like a dolphin. And she was purple. And annoyed. "The guardian demons said you could help us—the gwygii—" Seven stuttered, her teeth chattering so hard she thought they might all crack and fall out. And her dad would kill her because the bill to fix them would be horrendous.

"Get in the water. Get behind me."

Oh. So Nessie apparently spoke in one's head, not out loud like a normal mythical being.

Haran immediately waded into the water, which meant that she wasn't picky about speaking only to her own kind—she included humans, too. Nice of her, really.

But Seven *hated* water. Which was ironic, since she was going to help save a world that was completely under the water. She didn't like to touch it. She panicked if it got above her waist, so much so that she felt like she was drowning even before her head went under. She stood frozen on shore as Haran waded to almost his chest and then started swimming.

"Hurry, banshee. The demons are upon us."

Seven turned quickly, shoving her flaming hair out of the way so she could see around it. Nessie did not lie. The gwygii had reached the grassy slope down to the loch, and they snarled and leaped toward her with a hungry eagerness that would have her screaming in her sleep for life, she was sure.

She raced into the water. They followed, but were too slow. When Seven had compared Nessie to a dinosaur, she had been wrong. Unless dinosaurs had the ability to shoot a steady stream of ice from their mouths. Nessie roared, a sound that Seven felt shake her very bones, and the entire loch seemed to respond. The water around them surged and plummeted in great waves. A whirlpool formed way out in the center, but Seven only got a quick glance at it before she was knocked under the surface by the frozen force of Nessie's blast. She gasped, inhaling lungfuls of water, before she felt Haran—her sweet little brother who knew how afraid of water she was, grabbing at her, pulling her up, up out of the abyss she was flailing through.

She surfaced and sucked in air, choking and coughing and hacking up more than half her lung, by the feel of it. "Did you see that? Did you see what she just did?" Haran yelled, apparently unaware that his sister was suffering severe and traumatic water stress. He was so excited he was bouncing, even as waves washed completely over their heads. "She blew ice and froze them all up! The whole pack!"

"Now would be a good time to sing your song, banshee."

Seven splashed back up to shore, scrubbing

loch water from her eyes. Haran had been right. The entire pack stood frozen in the grass. The scream came easier to Seven now—she didn't even have to dig for it. It was just *there*, waiting for her.

The pack shattered into a gazillion shards of ice and demon. It rained down around her, getting in her hair, embedding in her clothes. Nessie retreated into the loch, and Seven, with no choice other than being impaled or blinded by frozen demon bits, followed her.

"The doorway is open, young ones. Hold on to my neck and I will take you there." Nessie bowed her long neck gracefully toward them. Seven wrapped her arms around it immediately, grateful for something solid to hold. She could feel the cold seething outward from the ice inside the sea creature, and yet for the first time since she'd seen Death staring down her little brother, she felt safe.

Until they reached the whirlpool.

"Swim to the middle. The tunnel lies within."

Swim to the middle? Of a whirlpool? Suddenly, Seven wasn't quite so fond of Nessie.

Haran, however, didn't hesitate. He let go and kicked through the water like he was part fish. Straight to the whirlpool. And Seven couldn't let him go alone—whatever lay beyond, they would face it together. She reluctantly let go of Nessie. "Thank you! Thank you so much!" she yelled, hoping to be heard above the roar of the water.

Nessie winked, and if sea monsters could smile, she was surely doing it.

Seven turned her back, following Haran. She swam awkwardly and slow—more doggy paddle than Olympic swimmer. It was hard enough swimming through the waves, but when she hit the whirlpool, that's when the fun really started.

By fun, she totally meant horror.

It grabbed her and spun her around. Over and upside down—she wasn't even sure she was above water most of the time. She tried to scream but water filled her mouth and choked her. She tried to cry but water stole her tears. She couldn't see Haran; she couldn't see anything.

CHAPTER FIVE:
AN UNDERGROUND
TUNNEL, WORMS, AND
DINOSAUR BONES.
WHAT FUN!

The whirlpool sucked her in, dragging her down, down, down. She flailed and kicked, but she could not fight her way to the surface—the pull was too strong. Just when she was positive she was going to die, and she hadn't even seen Death coming, the whirlpool dropped her flat on her back into a tunnel.

She groaned as she pushed herself to a sitting position. "You okay, Haran?" She blinked, trying to get water out of her eyes.

Her brother was bouncing. Positively bouncing.

"That was awesome! And look, Sev! The tunnels—they're see-through!" Haran ran to the nearest wall and pressed his face against it. "Look! There's a whole bunch of worms!"

Seven stared around them, completely in awe. The tunnel walls were indeed see-through. Above her, she could see the loch, and Nessie—in the distance. For a brief moment, panic nearly overwhelmed her at the thought of all that water—what if the tunnel collapsed?

"Oooh. Is that a skeleton?" Haran yelled and raced down the tunnel several feet, pointing up.

"The loch is deep and is the habitat of an ancient sea monster, Haran. I'm sure there are many skeletons."

"Wow. You mythical creatures get all the good stuff."

Seven smirked and finally talked herself into getting off her butt. The tunnel floor was covered in soft grass, which made absolutely no sense because there was no sun or water to make it grow. But then again, it was created by magic, so who was she to be confused? She followed Haran down the tunnel, craning her neck to look up.

"Yep. That is indeed a dead body. How fun. Shall we go?" She took his arm and led him away.

They walked for hours. With each step they took, the land above seemed to speed by, and Seven slowly realized that the time-space continuum in the tunnel was not the same as on land. If she was right in her guess, walking for an hour in the tunnel would be like several hundred hours on land. Which meant . . . she had absolutely no idea where this tunnel would lead them. Or whom they might meet along the way.

"I'm getting hungry," Haran said in a small, tired voice. They hadn't eaten since lunch time at school . . . yesterday. Probably twenty-four hours by now. No wonder he sounded exhausted and she felt weak and cranky.

"I have granola bars in my bag. And juice boxes." She smiled and ruffled his hair. "And we probably need to sleep. I don't know what we'll have to be prepared for when we find the end." *If we find the end.* Claustrophobia nearly choked her. She shoved it away. The guardian demons needed her. They wouldn't send her in here if there was a chance she wouldn't find her way out before she died of hunger.

Their packs were still soggy. Her tablet was long since ruined, but her dad had put her cell phone in a water-proof case before she'd packed it. He was a genius. The only problem was, it was dead and as far as she could tell, there wasn't a power source in the tunnels. She tucked it back inside. Then she tugged all their clothes out and laid them across the grass to dry. Haran collapsed on the ground next to them, leaning against the tunnel wall. He stared with glassy, exhausted eyes at the land above them—they'd left the loch behind hours and hours ago—and now she could distinctly see the outline of dinosaur bones. If she had any idea where they were, she would write to some archeologists when she got home and let them know.

"Here. This will help. Then we'll sleep, okay?" she sank down next to him, handing him the boxed lunch their dad had somehow snuck into Haran's backpack. It was full of sandwiches and carrot sticks and cookies. Way better than granola bars.

"What if we don't get out?" Haran asked, his

voice still small and scared.

Seven sighed, pulling him over so he leaned against her shoulder. "Well. If we don't find the end and you think it's time to go, I will figure out how to use my laser eyes and I'll cut us a path right out of here."

"You think?" he asked around a yawn.

"Yes, Haran. If that's what it takes so you're not scared, that's what I'll do."

He was quiet for a long time. She thought he'd gone to sleep when he finally said, "I think your laser eyes would be better than your scream. If you screamed, the tunnel might collapse and smoosh us."

Seven chuckled. "Yeah. You're probably right."

He started to snore almost before Seven finished her sentence. The temperature in the tunnel was warm, thank goodness, because they had nothing even passably blanket-like. She pulled her hoodie off and wadded it into a ball for a pillow before pushing Haran over on it. He didn't even stir. She watched him sleep for several minutes, wondering if she would make it before

Death found him. Wondering if she wasn't leading him right to Death's arms. Wondering if he'd ever see their father again. Her heart ached, and for the first time since they'd left, she felt tears soak her cheeks. She scrubbed them away, sniffling. Being a banshee was hard. Being a big sister was harder.

She tried to stay awake, to keep guard. Like a real banshee, protecting her charge. But she wasn't a real banshee, she was half-human. And she was too tired. She lost the battle with sleep not long after Haran did.

She awoke with a start to the sound of feet reverberating through the tunnel. Panicked, she jerked upright, spinning, already digging for her banshee half. The creatures coming around the bend, however, were far more frightened of her than she was of them. "Banshee!" the first centaur screamed, stumbling backward, his horse tail whipping the centaur behind him. "Banshee!

Run! Run before she kills us all!" Over and over, they screeched, but there were too many of them, and they were stuck in the tunnel. A centaur traffic jam.

Seven glanced at Haran, hating the way the flush of shame crept up her neck. She wasn't evil. She wasn't a killer. She was a guide. A comforter. Why couldn't anyone see that? And how did they even know she was a banshee anyway? Lots of people had red hair and green eyes, not just banshees.

"Seven?" Haran asked, his eyes wide as he stared at her.

"It's okay, I don't think they'll hurt us—"

"Seven, you're flying."

"What?" She looked down at the ground, several feet below her. With a screech that shook the tunnel, she crashed down, landing hard and rolling twice before she came to a rest at the centaur's feet. "Haran!" she cried, whirling around and crawling back to him. "Did you see that? I flew!"

Haran grinned. "Yeah. I think I was the one who pointed it out."

The centaurs stared at her in something that seemed to be a mix of horror and confusion. "She's a good banshee," Haran offered. "We're just trying to get out of this tunnel."

"We, too, wish to leave this tunnel. How far is it to the other end?" The first centaur, the one she'd scared so badly, stepped forward, watching her with narrowed, suspicious eyes. But Haran, he seemed to trust. Which was understandable. Her little brother was adorable.

"Hours and hours and hours. Maybe days. I don't know." Haran shrugged. "How long 'til we reach your end?"

The centaur smiled. "Less than an hour."

Haran's entire face lit up and he jumped to his feet. Seven grabbed him and they yelled, jumping in circles. They would live. They would escape this tunnel. And she could *fly*. Somehow, begging her banshee half for help so often seemed to have let loose powers she hadn't realized she really had. And now they seemed eager to make their presence known. She leapt into the air, felt her bones lighten, her legs fading gradually until it looked like she was nothing but a ghost—except for the top half of her, which was still decidedly human. "Haran! Let me see if I can carry us both!"

He jumped and caught her hand. She tugged him, willing them to fly higher. It was a struggle. She wobbled in the air like a badly-thrown football, but then she felt it, the surge of her banshee half rising to the surface to give her the strength her human half didn't have. They soared around the tunnel, over the frightened centaurs, then back again. "Let's pack up our stuff and get out of here!" she laughed, dropping him to the ground and landing next to him. Her feet, thankfully, reappeared, jeans and sneakers and all.

"Where do you travel to?" the centaur asked, approaching her cautiously.

She looked up, wanting to glare at him for judging her without knowing her at all, but it wasn't in her. Instead, she smiled and tried to be reassuring. "I'm not sure. Atlantis, eventually. To open the gate so people can defeat some bad guy named Phoibos."

"We were exiled from there. They're purging all the hybrids." He looked pointedly at her very human self.

"I've heard. But sometimes," she tipped her head to the side, considering her own words as she spoke them. Her eyes flitted to Haran, shoving everything in his pack. "Sometimes, we have no choice but to run right into danger. Or we risk losing everything worth fighting for."

Haran looked up with a wide smile. "She's also a philosopher. Bet you never met a banshee who was all *that*, did you?"

"This human—?"

"He's my little brother. I'm taking him to the Fountain of Youth."

The centaur's eyes widened and he looked at Haran more closely. "But he's so young—"

"Death follows him," Seven said quietly.

The half-horse man's lips formed a silent *O*, and he nodded. "I am sorry for our reaction. All banshees are not kind, as you are."

"I've only met my mother. She's . . . not mean. She's not nice. She's not anything." Seven shrugged.

"Six took my mother to Death. So she didn't have to go alone." Haran stood and slung his bag over his shoulder. "Six isn't evil. Neither is Seven. Maybe no hybrids are."

Seven smiled sadly. Haran had been a baby when his mother, Erin, had died. It was the first time Seven had ever met her mother, because the mighty Six, after giving birth, had decided human life wasn't for her and had given it up forever. And she'd left. When Seven was two, her dad had met a wonderful woman who loved them both so much. They were happy. Haran was the little brother Seven prayed for every night. But when he was nine months old, almost walking, his mother got sick.

It was the first time Seven had seen Death.

For days, she sat with her step-mother, staring out the window. She watched the black cloud on the horizon, wondering when it would get there. When the storm would arrive. But no one else could see it. No one else but Six.

Six followed it, because it was coming to her old village and she feared for Seven's dad's life. She came just as Death did, and she mourned, and she held Erin's hand as she died, and Dad had said goodbye. But Seven, she had seen Six holding Erin's soul. She had seen Death in his long black robes appear in the bedroom, red eyes just visible beneath the folds of his cloak. He had looked at her and nodded politely, acknowledging that he knew she saw him, and then he had held out his hand. Six had hugged Erin and whispered something Seven hadn't heard, and then she'd taken her hand and handed her to Death. He had gently led her away.

And Six went to Dad, put one ghostly hand to his cheek and then was gone. Not once did she even look at the tiny daughter so desperate for her mother's attention.

"Seven." Haran seemed to sense her thoughts, and he tugged gently on her hand. "Seven, it's okay now. You have me. And you have Dad."

She forced a smile, belatedly realizing tears were soaking her cheeks. "I do." She nodded, sniffling. "Let's go find that Fountain. Atlantis can't be that far away, can it?" She forced a cheerful grin.

The centaur frowned. "The Fountain isn't in Atlantis. The Fountain is on an island outside of

Japan. And this tunnel only leads you to Egypt."

"What?" Seven asked. Akie had never specifically told her they were going straight to the Fountain, she'd just assumed, but still . . . "Can I get to Japan from Egypt?"

He smiled gently, sensing her inner panic, and he nodded, his horse tail whipping back and forth absently. She'd seen real horses do it to brush away flies. She wasn't sure why a centaur would have need to do it, though. "There is a tunnel. It goes from Egypt to Zimbabwe. Once there, take the tunnel from Zimbabwe to the island. But beware. The island houses an active volcano. You should be able to make it in two days' walk. Less, if you can find someone to lend you their scooters."

"Scooters?" Seven asked because of everything he'd just told her, that was the only thing her mind would comprehend.

He nodded. "We must go. Good luck on your travels, brave one. And you, little human." Haran waved and Seven stepped aside, numb and yet hurting all at once, and watched them go. Two days? Two different tunnels? A volcano?

How on earth would she protect Haran through all of that?

"It's okay, Seven. We can do this. We can do this together." Haran nodded encouragingly and handed over her backpack. He must have re-packed while she wasn't looking.

She sucked in a deep breath and shoved her curls away from her face. She straightened her spine and forced a grin. "Yes. Okay. I can do this, Haran. As long as I have you, I can do this."

CHAPTER SIX:
MY MOTHER,
THE BANSHEE

etting out of the tunnel was decidedly easier than getting in. A ladder, simple and made of smooth wood, led to an opening in the top. Seven absently wondered how the centaurs got up and down ladders, but since she'd ditched them, she had no one to ask. "Ready for this?" She looked at Haran over her shoulder as she put her hands on the middle rung.

"I am. Are you? You got your banshee super powers ready, just in case?"

Was that fear she heard in her fearless brother's voice? Her heart hurt again, because he was too little for this journey. Too little to be facing Death. Too little to be fighting demons. But she plastered a bright smile on her face and turned to face him. "Yep. Locked and loaded. Let's get out of here!"

She pushed the latch aside and raised the doorway. Sand rained down on their heads and she coughed and sputtered and rubbed at her eyes before she dared poke her head out. It was daytime in Egypt. And *hot*. She'd never felt heat like this in Ireland. "Holy crap," she gasped, struggling to pull herself up and into the sand.

Haran followed, yelping when his fingers hit the heat. "What is *wrong* with this place? It's on fire!"

"It's the desert. I think it's supposed to be this hot. But look, Haran." She pointed around them in a sweeping motion. "Look at these."

Pyramids. Great, ancient pyramids surrounded them. Haran's eye got really wide and he spun in a circle, taking it all in. "Holy crap."

Seven smiled. There was the Haran she knew and loved.

He took off, running to put his hand against one, jerking back as it scalded his palm. And then he sprinted across the desert to the next one and did the same thing. She watched him, laughing when he didn't learn his lesson the first time, until something on the horizon caught her eye.

A black cloud. Coming closer. Coming for Haran.

"Haran, come on! We've gotta figure out where the next doorway is!" He must have heard the panic in her voice because he came straight back and grasped her hand. "Sorry. I mean, it's really hot, and I don't want us to get heat stroke." She tried to reassure him.

He didn't buy it, she could tell, but he pretended too. She could see a city in the distance, and decided they should head there first because she had no idea what else to do. She trudged across the sand, only going about twenty yards when a shadow formed in front of her.

She screamed, pushing Haran behind her, and the shadow blew to pieces.

"That was Akie!" Haran yelled.

"Oh my gosh. I killed Akie again!" Seven tried to grab at the bits she could still see, but they weren't solid anymore. Horrified, she watched as the pieces wafted on the non-existent breeze. And then they re-formed into Akie.

"You're not dead!" she squealed. He quickly sidestepped the force of her voice with an annoyed glare.

"Being torn apart does not kill a shadow. We're torn apart all the time."

"That sounds . . . unpleasant." She shuddered. *Ouch.*

"We must get you to the next tunnel, quickly. Demons can't get into the tunnel, little banshee. It's in the pyramid." He pointed, ushering them quickly and Seven turned, stumbling through the sand.

"Why? What's wrong? Are there demons here?"

"Many. Some with the face of a friend. Hurry, banshee!"

But she wasn't fast enough. Around them, shadows rose in a circle, locking them in. More guardian demons. She looked at Akie, standing behind them. His red eyes dulled and his head hung, chin resting on his chest in defeat. What was going on? And in the distance, the black cloud roiled closer. "We need to get to the tunnel. What are you doing?" she asked, turning slowly. They were completely blocked in.

The big one behind her spoke first, and she whirled so she could face him. "You were going to the wrong gate."

"Oh. Okay, which gate do I go to? I need to get him to the Fountain of—"

"No."

The single word made her blood run absolutely cold. She swallowed hard as Haran whimpered next to her. "No? What do you mean, no? Death is right there!" She pointed to the horizon, realizing belatedly that they couldn't see the cloud. And also, that she'd just shown Haran exactly how close he was to dying.

His face was completely white; his dark eyes round pits of terror. And he shook as he stared where Seven had pointed. He couldn't see it, but she could guess he was imagining it.

"Save Atlantis first. Then you may return to the Fountain."

"We don't have time! If I go to Atlantis, Death will catch us," she yelled. They shook and their shadows vibrated, but did not break.

"If you go to the Fountain first, you will not go to Atlantis."

Seven felt anger, unfamiliar and hot and broiling, surge through her blood. "Did your seer tell you that? You're guardian demons. You're supposed to be loyal to the thing you're guarding!"

"They aren't guarding us, Seven," Haran said quietly, inching closer to her side. "They're guarding Atlantis."

Not all of them. Akie had tried to help her. But she had moved too slowly. She met his eyes now, but they were dull and lifeless.

"I will *not* go to Atlantis unless I save my brother first." She planted her hands on her hips and glared at the big shadow.

"We assumed you would say that. Which is why we will take your brother and *keep him safe,*" his words seemed to writhe with venom, "until you return."

"What? No! No, you can't do that!" she reached for Haran's arm, but they were faster, slithering along the sand and erupting around him, knocking her away.

"Seven!" he screamed.

Screamed.

Fury unlike anything Seven had ever known shot through her and she sucked in a mighty breath.

Akie's hand covered her mouth, taking the force of her scream. She felt his entire body spasm in response to the pain, but he didn't move.

He was against her, too. Somehow, this knowledge hurt worse than all the other betrayals together.

"No, little banshee! If you scream, you will hit him, too!"

Seven froze, her mouth dropping as her entire body seemed to go limp. She'd almost killed her brother. Trying to save him, she'd almost killed him. "I'm a monster," she whispered.

"Seven!" Haran screeched.

"Use your lasers! Call the dead!" Akie hissed.

Haran screamed and screamed, fighting with his small hands and fists, but it didn't even faze them.

Seven tried. She focused on her eyes, told them to do something. They did not. In her mind, she scrolled through all the dead she'd taken and protected, but none of them appeared. And then Haran was gone. "I will do what I can for him," Akie said, and he was gone, too.

She sank to the sand, covering her face in her hands. She knew where they'd taken him, because she could see the cloud, Death's cloud, following them. But what could she do? The sobs shook her entire body, and she felt lost and alone. She'd failed. She'd failed Haran.

"Get up, Seven. We do not mourn the dead before they are gone."

Seven jerked up, scrabbling backward on her hands and feet like a crab. Six, in all her ethereal glory, balanced in the air in front of Seven, watching her with such sad, sad eyes.

"Mom?" Seven whispered.

Six had Seven's same fiery hair, except as a full banshee, hers was transparent. The same wide green eyes and milky white skin. Six was beautiful. So beautiful Dad had once described her as painful to look at, but more painful to look away *from*.

"Seven, I am so proud of you. You have come so far."

Seven choked on a cry. "You're—you're proud of me? But you don't even know me! You haven't seen me since I was three years old! You don't care at all! You wouldn't even look at me the last time I saw you. Or ever." She hadn't meant to say that last part, but she didn't regret it, either.

"It hurts, Seven. It hurts to see you because it reminds me of what I had to give up."

Seven could start a whole book on pain and why Six was not the one who was suffering, but suddenly, she didn't care. None of it mattered, not with Haran gone. So instead she asked the other, less important questions. "And what are you doing out of Ireland? Banshees don't leave Ireland!"

"I'm following you. You needed me, and I am here."

She said it with such a simple conviction that for several seconds, Seven couldn't speak.

"What?"

"Nate has done such an amazing job raising you that you did not need me until now, but I've always been there, Seven. Even when you couldn't see me, I was there. I can feel you. I feel your pain. I feel your joy. You are one of my souls, Seven, and I will never leave you. But until now, you have not needed me."

"Is that why you're here? To take me to Death?"

Six smiled gently. *"I'm here to help you save your brother."*

"They took him. They took him away and I couldn't save him and I almost killed him when I tried to save him and I failed him, Mom. I failed him." Seven started to sob again.

"Yes, you do need to get that screaming under control." Was Six smirking? Serene ghosts didn't smirk, did they? *"You have other tools at your disposal, Seven."*

"I tried them!" Seven threw her hands up, sand raining down on her head. "I don't know how to work them."

Six floated closer, until she was eye-level with her daughter. *"You were using your head. Your banshee half lives in your heart. You ask for help from there. And the souls, your army of dead will come when you call. They aren't mind readers, you know."* Six raised an eyebrow and grinned.

Her mother had a sense of humor. Who knew?

"But I can't scream. If I scream I blow everything up."

Six seemed to settle across from her, ghostly legs criss-crossed in front of her. *"Remember when you were little, and you used to sing songs to your imaginary friends?"*

Seven smiled at the memory, and then wondered how Six knew of it. Had she really been there all this time?

"Your imaginary friends weren't imaginary. They were your army of dead."

Seven felt goose bumps rise clear up to her scalp. Of *course* they were. How could she have not realized? There was Grandmother Macfarland, who was the second soul she'd ever taken, and Grandfather Bailey, who had been her first soul. They'd had tea parties with her.

Six watched her, pride written clearly across

her face as Seven was hit with the realization that she'd known how to call her army of dead before she'd known she *had* an army of dead. *"So now that you remember how to sing for them, let's work on those laser eyes so you can save your brother. I will distract Death for you."*

Seven stood up, straightened her spine and sucked in a deep breath. She could do this. She could go after Haran and she would take those shadows *down.* "Okay. How do I turn the lasers on?"

Six chuckled. *"Look for your banshee half in your heart. It's warm. That heat will fuel the flames from your eyes."* She paused, considering, and then continued, *"You're expecting lasers like in the movies. It isn't like that. It's more like leaping, protective fire. Picture it. Will the heat to warm your eyes. Focus internally, and the flames will come."*

Seven nodded and closed her eyes. She could feel her banshee half. She could feel the heat, something she'd always had but never realized that it was what made her a banshee. She grabbed it and pulled, trying to envision wavy flames exploding from her eyes, taking down her enemies. Her eyes felt warm, but not uncomfortably so, and when she opened them the flames sort of trickled out. They weren't waves, they were a light sprinkle that scalded her clothes.

Six laughed.

Seven scowled. "What did I do wrong?"

"When you envision it, tell me what you see."

"I see . . . big waves of flames taking down all the guardian demons."

Six nodded knowingly. *"Ah. There is your problem. When I said focus internally, I meant don't worry about what's outside of you. The flames will find them. Worry about the warmth. Inside. Focus on that."*

Seven took another deep breath—the eighth or ninth in the last several minutes, and tried again. As with her screaming, now that she knew where to find her banshee warmth, it was easier to grab it again. *Focus inside. Focus on the warmth.* She opened her eyes.

All she could see was fire, dancing, beautiful fire. She squealed, blinking several times, and the fire died. Her sight returned. "That was trippy."

Six smiled fondly. *"We must go. Death moves quickly. Are you ready, Seven?"*

Seven met her eyes, and the tears there told her everything. When they left, when Six went to distract Death, Seven would not see her again. And fighting to save her brother would be all up to her. Six couldn't be in two places at once, but Seven could see in those tears that her mother really, really wished she could.

When she said yes, she would lose her mother again. *No. Not again. I never lost her in the first place and I won't lose her now. She'll still be with me.* Seven blinked back tears of her own and nodded. "I'm ready."

CHAPTER SEVEN:
HOW TO KILL A SHADOW

Six waited until Seven was in the air before she followed her. The weird weightlessness was disorienting, and Seven wobbled a bit. *"One last bit of advice before I go?"* Six asked, looking worriedly toward the dark cloud quickly disappearing on the horizon.

"Of course," Seven gasped as she tumbled sideways. Six grabbed her wrist, her touch cold as ice, just before Seven hit the sand. "Thanks, Mom."

Six smiled. *"You're trying to control a physical body. But when you're in the air, you're a banshee. More than when you scream, more than when you have fire in your eyes, this is when you're more banshee than anything else."*

Seven closed her eyes—banshee half-humming, as if biding its time, waiting for the proper attention. Six spoke again, and Seven forced her eyes open. *"When you hand souls to Death, you don't do it on the ground. You leave your physical self behind to rise up to meet him. This is the same thing, Seven. You've done it sixty-three times already."*

Seven sobbed a little. Her mom knew how many souls she'd delivered. She really had been there all along. Yes, she'd done this before. She just hadn't embraced it like she should have. Nodding her agreement, she let go. Let go of her human half, let go of the fear and the sadness and the pain that were all holding her on the ground. And then she rocketed forward, flying past Six.

One short flight together. Seven glanced at her mother as they shot forward. She was beautiful; her bright hair streamed behind her and the tattered, ghostly train of her gown waved gently on the breeze, hiding her feet. And although there was a steely determination in her face, there was also peace. Joy. They soared through the sky, so fast they left a wind tunnel behind them, so fast that the ground, the people, the endless sand, it was all a blur. They were nearly upon the guardian demons—Seven could see them in the distance. She spun like a bullet, her arms stretched out like a superhero, going faster and faster. Her mother's delighted laugh was the last thing she heard before Six veered away toward the cloud.

Toward Death.

Seven continued on her own path, feeling as if half her soul was torn and following Six. And yet, her heart had healed. All these years of feeling abandoned and hurt and ignored, they had shattered her a little. And just like that, Six had smoothed the shards back into place and given Seven the courage to be who she needed to be.

Not human. Not a banshee. She was a hybrid, and she was powerful enough to save her brother.

The demons had a sort of temporary camp set up. There were no fortifications, no guards. They clearly thought she was going to scamper off and do their bidding. And why wouldn't they? She'd never stood up to anyone or anything in her life. But they'd taken her brother and awoken the banshee side in her that the myths were made of—the side everyone was afraid of. This was the reason animals avoided her and magical creatures didn't come near her village in Ireland.

She had to be careful, because Haran was down there. And Akie. She had to be careful or she'd tear apart the whole camp. So Seven screamed, but not with too much fury—because she still couldn't see Haran and she didn't want to hurt him—and plus, she'd already learned her scream could knock them down but it didn't kill them. She watched in fascination as the sound waves split the air and roared toward their camp. It hit the first three demons and knocked them backward. They sprawled on their back as the other four sprang to their feet, running out of the tents. She landed right in the middle of them, hard, so that the ground split at her feet and shook away from her like a mini-earthquake.

Well. Mom didn't mention that.

The demons running at her fell over the ground waves, while the first three still lay unconscious at her feet.

Haran, where are you?

Since screaming again was out, she called on the warmth, feeling it rush through her, almost taking on a life of its own as the flames rolled from her eyes and sought their target. She really, really hoped Haran was out of the way.

The demons screamed, and she realized she *could* see through the flames. Everything was distorted and blurry, but she found the only remaining Egyptian guardian on his feet and attacked. The shadow melted away into liquid blackness in the sand. She blinked rapidly, calling back the heat, until she could see clearly again. No one moved.

Her sneakers slid in the sand as she spun on her heel and ran for the tents. "Haran?"

There was no answer.

Her throat closed. Had she been too late? Had Death made it here before she did? She jerked back the flap, almost afraid of what she would see, but there was no adorable little brother waiting inside. It was empty. She tried the next tent, and the next, but he wasn't there. She stormed out, headed for one of the first demons she'd hit with her scream, and nudged him with her foot. "Wake up."

When he didn't stir, she pushed harder. "Wake up! What did you do with my brother?" He moaned, and she watched in morbid curiosity as his shadow body put itself back together, gathering darkness from around him.

"We did nothing with your brother, you evil little human. He's in the tent."

"No. No he's not," Seven growled, shocked at her own aggressiveness. The demon's eyes widened and he looked behind him, toward the still slightly smoldering tents. He really didn't know where Haran was. She spun in a circle, watching with dismay as the other demons slowly started to reform. The puddles, they weren't moving so well—it would be a while. But the other two were already struggling to their feet.

She had to find Haran. Fast.

She started again toward the tent, but one of the guardian demons blocked her. The other two raced off in the opposite direction. It took her confused brain about ten seconds to realize her brother had escaped, and they had found his scent. The demon reached for her, but she sprang into the air, out of reach, and shot after the two racing across the sand.

There, in the distance, was a big black shadow carrying a small boy. At first, Seven thought he was carrying him back to camp, but no—he was running away from them.

Akie. He'd saved her brother. Now she could see that he was making a direct line to the pyramids, and the tunnel. The two running after him wouldn't catch him—he had too big of a lead, but neither he nor Haran could do a thing with a magical doorway once they got there. They would be trapped. She risked a glance over her shoulder. The rest of the guardian demons were on their feet, some already in pursuit. When Akie had said they guard their target no matter what, he hadn't been kidding. They were charged with getting her to Atlantis, and it seemed they weren't going to stop until they did.

But she couldn't kill them. They just reformed when she screamed or attacked them with fire. What could she do? She put on a burst of speed and shot ahead, twisting and riding on air currents to propel her forward. She roared over the two in the lead, the wind from her blast nearly knocking the giant shadows over. "Akie! Haran!" she cried when they were within hearing distance.

"Seven! I knew you'd come!" Haran waved like this was all a grand adventure. Like it hadn't ripped her heart completely out of her chest when he'd been taken.

She swung down, keeping pace with them. "Of course I would come. How'd you escape? No wait-tell me later. Akie, how do I stop them?"

He looked over at her, red glowing eyes dim. "I don't think you can, little banshee."

Haran's face lit up. "Did you use the lasers?"

"Yes, but they reformed." Seven's heart sank. Was there no way to stop them?

"What about the army? Did you call your dead?"

Akie skidded to a halt. "Your dead. Your army."

"Yeah," Seven said, landing next to him. This time she didn't crack the ground or send waves rolling away or anything. If she didn't know better, she'd think she was getting the hang of this. "I have an army. I know how to call them. But even if they attack, it doesn't do us anything but buy a little time."

"Your dead have access to the underworld. They can take my companions back to the fiery pits we escaped from." Akie stared hard across the sand. "They can return us to our dungeon."

"Not us, Akie. Them." Seven nodded, licking her dry, cracked and burned lips. "I'll meet you at the pyramids. Go!"

Akie hesitated, looking from the oncoming demons to Seven and back again. Seven shooed at him with her hands. "You told me that all demons aren't evil. You don't belong there, Akie."

"You can live with us!" Haran exclaimed. Seven snickered. Akie, for the first time ever, smiled. And then he turned and ran, Haran tucked under his arm.

Seven closed her eyes, shutting them out, trying to let go of her human half. And then she started to sing. The words were ancient Celtic lyrics. She didn't know what most of them meant, and she didn't know how she'd learned them. Her dad certainly hadn't taught her.

Six. Six must have sung it to her while Seven wasn't aware of it. When she was sleeping. As she started to sing, she remembered. She remembered the very vivid dreams of her mother leaning over her bed, brushing her bright curls away from her face, and singing softly.

They hadn't been dreams.

She sang, the words dancing from her tongue and carrying on the breeze. At first, nothing happened. But Six had told her they would come, and she was so done doubting her mother. So she kept singing.

She didn't realize they were there until she was suddenly surrounded. Many more than the sixty three souls she'd taken—apparently they'd brought friends. They arrived just as the first two demons reached her. "Umm. Can you—can you take them back to their dungeon?" she asked, because her army watched her, oblivious to the creatures who were fighting their way toward her now.

Grandmother Macfarland laid a gentle, icy

hand against her cheek with a smile. The others, though, leaped forward, surrounding the two guardian demons. Seven could see the shadows fighting, but they were fighting a battle they could not win. Her ghosts couldn't be hurt. It took a couple dozen of them, but they dragged them down, down into the sand and then through it.

And they were gone.

"There are more coming. We have to stop them—they're trying to take my brother."

"Keep singing, child. We will accompany them."

Seven nodded, singing quietly, but her voice rose in pitch as the rest of the guardian demons came close. She sang faster, urging her army on, and they raced ahead with a fierce battle cry, fists raised.

They swarmed the demons, rising over the top of them, gripping the shadows with their ghostly hands and pulling them away, into the sand and then under where Seven couldn't see them. "Will the souls be okay?" she asked Grandmother Macfarland.

The old ghost smiled, her eyes crinkling at

the corner. "Yes."

"Thank you. Thank you so much. You've saved my brother—"

"I think there are more. I feel the evil nearby," Grandfather Bailey said.

"Yes, there is. But he's a friend."

Grandfather shook his head. "No, another one. They're together."

Seven felt like she'd been punched in the stomach. "Oh no. The big one. The leader—I didn't see him when I attacked the camp. He must have known I'd go after Haran—I bet he's waiting at the pyramid! Akie's running right into a trap!"

"Go, Seven. We will follow."

"Thank you," she cried as she leaped into the air. Her heart raced in her chest as she flew across the sand. She pushed herself as fast as she could go, so fast she felt her skin pull tight, but when she landed next to the pyramid, it hadn't been fast enough. She was too late.

The big shadow had Akie by the throat with one hand, and Haran by the throat with the other hand. Haran held tight to the creature's arm, his feet kicking helplessly.

"Let them go." Her voice surprised her. She sounded strong and sure, not trembling and afraid.

He looked over at her, his eyes bright red. "I told you to go to Atlantis."

"Not without my brother. Let them go." Haran's face was turning an alarming shade of blue. And even as her ghosts gathered behind her—she could feel their strength and their anger—she couldn't send them after the big demon without endangering Akie as well. He did not deserve to go back to the dungeon.

Mom? What do I do? How do I save them?

She could almost swear she heard her mom answer her in head. *You're a banshee, Seven.*

Right. So she was.

Haran hadn't seen her laser eyes yet. It was time she showed him. Sucking in a breath, because she was still learning control and one wrong move would make her hit her brother. She squeezed her eyes shut and called the fire.

Her eyes flew open, the flames exploding. She stared hard at the sand at her feet until she could see, and then she raised her head, the flames leaving a trail of molten puddles straight to the big demon's feet.

He screamed, dancing backward. Seven's eyes started to burn, but she couldn't blink. Not yet. She followed him, not daring to breathe or move her head, until she caught his feet. Then she jerked her head up and the lasers set him on fire.

He shrieked, dropping Haran and Akie both as he pounded at the flames. "Akie, run!" Seven screamed. Akie grabbed Haran and ran in the opposite direction. The big demon reached for them, but he was too late. "Get him!" Seven cried.

Her ghosts surged forward, smothering him and dragging him down, just like all the others. He was bigger and stronger and it took more of her ghosts to do it. He managed to throw a few off, and Seven screeched as they toppled into the pyramid. Did it hurt them? Were they okay?

More joined the fight, piling on top of him until he was forced into the sand. His hands clawed the air, but it did no good. There was nothing to grab, and then he was gone. Back to his cage.

Seven rubbed at her eyes, looking for Grandfather Bailey. "Are they gone? Was that the last of them? Are the ghosts going to be okay?"

"Yes." He smiled gently. "They are safe and so are you. Now we return to the beyond until you need us."

Grandmother Macfarland again laid a hand to her cheek, and Seven leaned into it, feeling grateful tears filling her burned eyes. "Thank you. All of you. Thank you so much. How about next time, we just have a tea party again instead of an epic battle?"

This amused her army. Some of them chuckled, some smiled. And then they faded away with raised hands in farewell. "Good bye," Seven whispered.

She watched until there was nothing left but torn, imprinted sand. Then she went to find her brother. "Haran? Akie?" she yelled, wandering among the pyramids. She was getting close to the tourist section now, and people milled around, looking at the battered, exhausted, lost girl curiously.

"Seven!" Haran yelled, crashing through people like a miniature bulldozer. He threw himself into her arms and she hugged him tight. "I knew you could do it. I knew you had magic powers."

Seven cried. She wasn't sure if she was crying from relief or exhaustion or belated fear, but she cried until the top of Haran's head was soaked.

"Hey, Seven? Do you still have food? I'm starving."

Seven laughed through her tears. "I left our packs over there before I came after you. Let's go see if they're still waiting for us." Haran let her go and skipped off. He was such a brave, brave little boy. So much braver than she was. "Where's Akie?" she asked, jogging to catch up to him.

"He's around here somewhere."

"I'm here, little banshee." Akie appeared next to her, rising up out of the sand.

She stared around them worriedly. There were still tourists everywhere. "Aren't you afraid someone might see you?"

He shook his head. "To them, I look like a trick of the light. Sometimes, humans see us, but they think it's their tired eyes or a figment of their imagination. When something is so horrifying, the mind makes excuses to protect itself from fear."

"You aren't horrifying. You're fun," Haran said, still skipping. "Look! There they are!" He raced to their packs, ripping them open and digging through them before Seven and Akie even got there.

"Do you eat?" she asked Akie.

He gave her an amused smile. "I eat the light."

Oh. Well then, she guessed she didn't have to worry about feeding *him*. Haran, on the other hand, was looking at their sensible sandwiches and granola bars with extreme distaste. "We need some real food."

Seven plunked herself down next to him, feeling the sand scald her legs through her jeans. The sun was setting, though, so hopefully it would cool down soon. "This is all we've got, kiddo. I have some money, but I think it won't work here."

Akie stood guard while they ate. Now that she and Haran weren't fighting for their lives and

Seven's stomach wasn't trying to devour her from the inside out, she was exhausted. Her eyes refused to stay open, no matter how hard she tried.

"Sleep. I will keep watch through the night," Akie said. Haran already leaned to the side, one second away from toppling on his face. Seven nudged him, pushing his pack under his head before he hit the ground.

"Are you sure? Do you get sleepy?" she asked, peering up at Akie in the quickly dimming light.

"No. Demons don't sleep."

She considered him while she fought with her eyelids. "Akie, you aren't a demon. You're a friend."

He smiled, his red eyes dimming. "Thank you, little banshee. I don't believe I've ever been called a friend before. Now sleep. The tunnel awaits you in the morning."

CHAPTER EIGHT:
SPHINX AND ANUBIS
AND SAND, OH MY!

The rising sun woke her, trying to blind Seven from the outside of her eyelids as the heat scalded her fair skin. Groaning, she sat up, rubbing her face and trying to untangle her hair. It was going to take at least a whole bottle of conditioner to get the tangles out of her curls.

"You never told me," she said around a yawn, finding Akie in the shadows next to her. "How did you escape with Haran?"

Haran grinned, his eyes still shut, but said nothing. Akie glanced at him in amusement. "I did not escape with Haran. He escaped with me."

Seven's eyebrows shot up as she climbed to

her knees. Holy crap she was *sore*. Fighting and running and flying and shooting flames did that to a girl, apparently.

"I was held captive for trying to help you. Haran dug his way out of his tent and let me free. They were sure you'd do as they said, so there were no lookouts. We were able to walk away while they entertained themselves."

"You—you saved yourself." Seven looked at Haran, pride giving her goose bumps up and down her neck. "You didn't even need me."

He sat up, frowning. "Yeah, 'cause the big guy at the end was totally going to let us go."

She ruffled his hair, brushing sand out of the silky strands. Then she dug for granola bars and juice boxes in their packs. "You could have handled him."

"I knew you'd come. I just thought maybe I'd help if I could." Haran shrugged, devouring his granola bar with a grimace. He'd never been a fan. Their dad usually sent him with fruit bars in his lunch, but they must have been out. That, or Haran had eaten them all while she wasn't looking.

Seven started packing their things back up. "Okay, so we'll just hop through the doorway and make it to the Fountain—" she said, glancing at Akie through the tangled wall of hair.

"I cannot go with you into the tunnel. They are magic, and demons can't go in." Akie watched them from the shadows of the pyramid they leaned against.

"But who will protect us? How will we survive without you?" Seven's throat tried to strangle her with fear. She swallowed it back, her entire body starting to shake.

He shook his head, and she could swear the red eyes rolled. "I don't know if you noticed, but you're the scariest thing out there. More powerful than one guardian demon."

She blinked twice, trying to register his words. She was more powerful than great big formidable Akie? Than the gwygii? "Thank you," she said, trying not to let him see the happy tears threatening to escape her still-sore eyes. She cleared her throat. "Can you go back to Ireland? And wait with my dad? Just in case—just in case anyone goes after him . . . "

He nodded, his eyes lighting briefly with hope. He had a purpose. A place to go. "Yes. Yes, I will do that."

Seven struggled to her feet, dusting her jeans off before she approached Akie. "Thank you. For everything. Travel safely, okay?"

He smiled, his eyes dimming and brightening and dimming and brightening. He most certainly did not look like a demon with the big, goofy grin on his face. "I will take care of your father, little banshee."

Haran hurled himself into Akie's stomach, hugging him tight. "I'll miss you!"

Akie stumbled back, his hands up like Haran might poison him. Slowly, so slowly, he lowered his hands to return Haran's hug. Seven bit her lip and tried not to cry. Again. A big, goofy grin matching Akie's split across her face.

They watched him fade into the shadows until he was completely gone. Then Seven nodded. "All right then. Shall we go? There's a tunnel in one of these pyramids that will take us to Zimbabwe."

"Nice. I hope it's cooler in Zimbabwe."

Haran brushed the back of his hand across his forehead, wiping away the sheen of sweat already beading despite the early hour of the day.

"You and me both, kiddo." Seven swung her pack on her back and started for the pyramid Akie had pointed to the day before. She glanced over her shoulder to see if Haran followed her.

Her eyes were immediately drawn to the horizon.

There, in the distance, was Death's black cloud.

"Yep. Time to go. Come on, Haran!" She grabbed his wrist and tugged him forward, jogging to the pyramid. She ducked inside the ancient door, relishing the cool interior. Who needed air conditioning when she could hang out in a centuries old tomb instead? She wandered around, dragging her fingers along the ancient blocks, until she felt the magic coursing from the wall in front of her. Okay, so that had to be the doorway. She walked up to it, expecting it to open.

It didn't.

"Now what?" Haran glanced around them in

confusion. "It's just a wall, Seven."

Seven frowned at him before glaring at the wall. "I don't know. I've never opened a magical doorway before. I thought—" A noise—the shuffle of footsteps—echoed off the wall and Seven spun, already screaming—not her death scream, but powerful enough that it hit a boy coming around the corner of the ancient tunnel and sent him flying through the air. He crashed into the wall and lay still.

Another boy stalked toward Seven, fists tight. "Hey! What did you do that for?" he yelled.

"I'm sorry. We've been attacked every time I turn around. I thought you were bad guys. I'm so sorry," Seven said.

Haran squinted at them. "How, exactly, do you know they *aren't* bad guys?" he asked quietly, so only she could hear. The one in front of them looked normal enough. Maybe thirteen, like her? Dark hair, hazel eyes. The guy lying on the ground looked like he was older than them, though. Maybe sixteen. Blond. Cute, if Seven wanted to notice. But she didn't want to notice right now, so she ignored it. Haran glanced at

Seven.

"You could have killed him." The boy bent down to check the other kid's pulse.

Haran smirked and Seven raised an eyebrow. "If I wanted to kill him, you would both be dead by now." Turning back to the blank wall, she said, "How does this doorway work?"

The boy looked up at her, confused. "You just go in."

"Go in what? It's just a wall," Haran said, throwing up his hands.

The boy seemed assured that his companion would live, and left his side to inspect the wall. "That's crazy. We came through here just a few hours ago."

Seven paced, nibbling on her thumbnail. "Something must be interfering." She thought back to the message on SplashSpace. The rumors that some guy named Phoibos was closing the gates. Maybe it was true. If they all shut, she'd lose her magic. She'd be human. Her mother would die.

She was still trying to process that particular, unsettling thought when a low rumble reverberated around them. Seven spun, immediately putting herself between Haran and whatever stood outside the pyramid walls. Cautiously, she stuck her head out the door. And didn't like what she saw.

Even without Haran's obsession with mythology his habit of telling her *everything* he learned, she would have recognized the sphinx right off. Giant creature made of sand, with the head of a human and a lion's body. She loved her riddles. And now she paced toward them, growling dangerously. Surrounding her were a gazillion Anubis-like creatures, their dog heads and human bodies made entirely of sand.

The boy whirled on her. "How do we do this? Do you know how to fight? I have powers but nothing that would help in battle."

Seven gave him a grim smile, *Yeah, I know how to fight.*

She glanced at the other boy just struggling to his feet behind them, blue eyes blinking as he rubbed the back of his blond head. Turning her back on him, she said to the other boy, "What's your name?"

"Colin." He blinked at her.

"What are your powers?" she asked, praying it would be something that could help them. His comment that he didn't have powers that would help in battle didn't inspire a lot of confidence.

"I have all the knowledge in the world because of a stupid fish. And a little magic here and there."

Her lips turned up in a slow smile. *Perfect.* "You take the sphinx. I'll take the rest." She darted through the square doorway of the pyramid, pausing just beyond. The first boy raced straight at the Sphinx, and she inwardly sighed. Were all boys so fearless?

The older boy finally joined them, standing just inside the door as he grimaced a bit at Seven. Then he looked at Haran, who still stood in the cool interior of the pyramid. "You're human, yes?"

With a resigned sigh, Haran said, "Yeah. I'm human."

"Then I'll protect you. Stay here where you're safe."

Haran frowned, clearly indignant. "I got this.

Go help your friend."

The guy hesitated and finally nodded. "I'm Cam, by the way."

"Haran. She's," Haran motioned toward her with his chin, "Seven."

Cam's eyes widened. "*The* Seven? The half-breed banshee?"

Several Anubis things had found them. They raced straight toward her, spears pointed at her chest. She didn't even have to dig very hard this time, the scream was there, waiting to be heard. The Anubis shattered into a billion grains of sand as the walls around Haran rained dust and sand on their heads. Cam nodded, agreeing with himself. "Yes. *The* Seven."

Haran slid past him, inching close to Seven. "Good luck."

"You, too."

Cam hurried after Colin and Seven turned to Haran. "Grab one of their spears. Stay away from them as much as you can." Haran nodded and scurried across the sand to grab two spears that had been left behind when she'd exploded the creatures.

She shot into the air and crashed down right in the middle of the bad guys. The force of the blast shattered many of the Anubises, their sand swirling in little tornadoes as more sand-dog-men fought their way through toward her. She called the heat and let the flames roll from her eyes, watching in satisfaction through her red haze as they melted into molten-colored puddles at her feet. If only she could scream again, it would take out most of them. But how, without hurting Colin, Cam, and Haran?

Suddenly her brother was at her side, swinging his spears like he'd been trained in martial arts. She caught sight of the horizon and the dark cloud. It was close. Too close. She blinked several times, clearing the heat from her eyes. "We don't have time for this," Seven muttered. "Haran, can you tell those boys to cover their ears? We need to get rid of these things and open that doorway!"

Haran nodded, turned, and ran off, weaving through the Anubises. He'd make a great cab driver one day. She heard him shout to the others, "Cover your ears!" They both stared at him, confused by what they apparently thought an odd request. Haran glared, motioning with his head toward where Seven watched them impatiently.

"Oh," Cam mouthed and clamped his hands over his ears. Colin copied him, and Haran dropped his spears so he could muffle the sound as well.

The scream was fueled by her panic this time, and as it tore from her throat she could feel that it was much more powerful than any of her screams before. The ground shook, the Anubises burst into poufs of dust, and the mighty Sphinx toppled over onto her side. Seven was knocked off her feet, crashing hard into the sand. She could hear Colin screaming about attacking her while she was down, but Seven couldn't see anything through all the dust.

Haran appeared like a little wraith through the mist, running to her side. "Are you okay? You stopped screaming—I thought—"

She coughed and tried to get up but she was half buried in sand. . He fell to his knees beside her as she pushed herself to her elbows, sputtering. "Don't . . . scream," she paused to choke for a second, "like a banshee . . . when you're surrounded . . ." more coughing, "by sand."

"I got the key! We can open the doorway!" Colin crowed, skidding to a halt next to them. "Cam needs to head back to Atlantis."

Cam stepped forward, offering his hand to help Seven to her feet. Haran rose, too, brushing sand from his hair. "May I accompany you?" Cam asked, glancing from him to Seven and back.

"Of course." Seven coughed. "I sorta owe you . . . for throwing you against the wall." She blushed, feeling more than a little bad about living up to a banshee's terrifying reputation— against a nice guy.

Cam inclined his head. "Thank you."

Colin grinned. "Hey! We rode here on scooters. We're supposed to take them back. Wanna borrow them?"

Seven looked at Haran, waiting for his confirmation. "It beats walking," he said with an excited grin.

"Yes, we would love that. Thank you."

CHAPTER NINE:
JUST A PINCH WILL DO IT

Where are we going?" Cam asked as Seven ran back to the pyramid. He jogged behind her, his long legs making it easy for him. Seven shoved her sand-saturated hair out of her face and risked a glance over her shoulder, meaning to see Cam. Instead, her eyes moved to the cloud. To Death.

"Zimbabwe," she said quickly, running faster. "They told me there's a tunnel there that goes to the Fountain of Youth." She looked over at Haran, who paled. Anubises he could apparently fight without batting an eye. Death, though, scared him. "Don't worry. I won't let him catch you."

"I need to go back to Atlantis," Cam said.

Seven nodded as she slipped inside the pyramid with Colin's key. She ushered Haran ahead of her and ran to the wall, laying the key against it. "Hurry hurry hurry." She bounced on her toes, nearly weeping with relief when the doorway shimmered to life. Without a second thought, she grabbed their bags and the scooters and shoved Haran through.

"Wait!" Cam called as the doorway began to shut. He frowned, looked around in panic and dove through. "This tunnel collapsed on us. I'm not sure how close to Zimbabwe we'll be able to get."

Seven's eyes fluttered shut in defeat. "Why?" she screeched. The walls shook and rocks crashed around them. Haran groaned.

Cam raised an eyebrow. "Perhaps because someone did something like that?"

She shuffled her feet, her hand clamped over her mouth lest she get any crazy ideas. "I'm still learning." She sank to the floor, her elbows on her knees and her head in her hands. "Death is chasing my little brother. I have to get him to the Fountain of Youth before Death catches us. And then I'll go to Atlantis. They told me this tunnel would take me to Zimbabwe, and then I could take a tunnel from there to the Japanese island where the Fountain is. Death can't get in the tunnel, so I thought we'd be safe."

Haran sat next to her and leaned on her shoulder. "It's okay, Seven. We'll still make it. We'll fly really fast."

Cam watched them silently until Seven nodded, raising her head. "Yes. We will. We'll make it. So. How do these scooters work?"

Scooters were way more fun than walking. They flew down the tunnel, which for the most part seemed just fine, except for bits of debris here and there. But the further they went, the worse it became, until narrowly avoiding fallen roof pieces or cracks in the floor morphed into a dangerous game of chicken.

Eventually, they had to give up the scooters because they spent more time climbing over blocked passageways than riding. "This is fun," Haran said. "It's like mountain climbing, except you're not going up."

Seven couldn't help but smile as she fought

with the rock currently blocking her path. Cam, with his long, strong legs, clambered easily over everything. Sort of like a mountain goat. Seven was not a mountain goat. Haran could be, if he wasn't so small. Maybe like a toddler mountain goat.

Haran would *so* smack her for calling him a toddler mountain goat.

"I don't think we can go much further. It looks like it is completely blocked up ahead," Cam said, studying the path before them from his higher vantage point.

Fear raced down Seven's spine. "We have to go on the surface? But bad guys hang out on the surface." She glanced at Haran and read the terror in his eyes. *Death* hangs out on the surface.

Cam gave her a bright smile. "Don't worry. We aren't far from the Zimbabwe tunnel. A couple of hours walking, is all."

Seven squinted at him, and then at the ceiling. "How do you know?"

"Because," he said, clambering easily over the next very large boulder, "I came through this tunnel this morning. The entrance isn't far from where it's blocked."

"Oh. Good. We can outrun—" *Death*— "bad guys for a couple of hours." She attempted to leap over the rock Cam had, tripped, and landed flat on her face. Haran giggled, and then cackled, until Seven leaned up to glare at him. He covered his mouth with his hand but his eyes still danced with mischief.

Cam helped her to her feet, trying to hide his smirk. "You know, you can fly."

She dusted herself off, rubbing her flattened nose. "Yes. I can fly."

"So . . . why did you just fall?"

She blinked at him. "I was walking, not flying. Well, climbing, I guess, not really walking—"

Cam raised an eyebrow, tugging on one of her wild curls. "But you can *fly*. Why didn't you fly when you started falling?"

Haran scampered over to them, sliding down the rocks on his heels like he was on a skateboard. "He's got a point, Sev. You never have to fall on your face again."

"I'm still learning. I only learned how to call

my banshee powers yesterday, you know." She brushed past them, attacking the boulders blocking the path.

"Wait, you only learned yesterday? Seriously?" Cam asked, helping her clear away the smaller rocks.

"Yep. And then she took on a whole group of Egyptian guardian demons to save me. *Then* she killed all the Anubises and knocked over the Sphinx."

Cam's eyes widened. "You've been busy."

Seven snorted. Busy was an understatement. They worked in silence for several minutes, Haran digging like a puppy while Cam used broken sticks and boards to try to jam into the crevices to jar the bigger boulders lose. Seven pulled smaller ones out, hoping to get lucky and loosen the whole thing. She was hot and sweaty and dusty and every single finger nail was broken when she finally sat back, discouraged.

She could scream, and attempt to break up all the rocks, but it risked bringing the already broken tunnel down on top of them. It was too dangerous. "We're not going to get through. We'll have to go up," she said, brushing her hair back from her forehead. Haran's head poked up from the whole he was working on, looking for all the world like a brown gopher, squinty eyes and everything. Seven burst out laughing until she couldn't breathe, holding her sides and gasping for air.

"You don't look all that banshee-ish right now either, you know," Haran grumbled, shaking his head as dust billowed around him.

Cam was already scaling the blockage. Seven stared up at him. "How do we get out?" Would she have to scream after all and break a way through? Maybe her laser eyes . . .

"There's a hole. Humans call them sink holes. They happen on the surface when one of our tunnels collapse. Come on, little ones."

"I'm not little," Seven muttered as she started after him, pushing Haran before her. "Why does everyone keep calling me little?"

Cam glanced over his shoulder. "Because you are. What are you, twelve?"

"Thirteen. I'm small for my age."

He grinned. "I see."

"And what are you? Old?" She squinted suspiciously at him. "And while we're at it, what kind of magical creature are you, anyway?"

He chuckled quietly as he found crevices for his fingers and toes, scaling the rocks. "I'm sixteen. And I'm an Atlantian guard. So not really magical. Just tough."

"Tough, huh?" Seven muttered. His foot just happened to slip and rained pebbles down on her head. She was pretty sure he'd done it on purpose.

They climbed the rest of the way in silence, except for calling out occasional warnings or offering help. By the time they made it to the top and climbed out onto more sand, Seven's arms were shaking and her hands were blistered. Her feet wanted to die. That was all there was to it.

Cam watched her massaging her legs for several seconds. "Why didn't you fly?"

"I didn't fall," she said, distracted as she surveyed the damage to her jeans. The holes in the knees of her pants were far from stylish. Now they were just big and gaping.

"No . . . but you had no reason to climb,"

Cam said slowly.

Seven's head snapped up. "I could have flown."

He pursed his lips and nodded.

"I could have carried Haran and you both out of there."

Cam frowned. "I don't know about me, but Haran, definitely."

Haran thunked himself on the ground at their feet. "She's super strong, dude."

She glared up at Cam, throwing her hands in the air. "And you waited until we were clear to the top to ask me this?"

Cam leaned down until they were face to face. "You're a banshee, but it doesn't come naturally to you. If you're going to survive Atlantis, you need to change that."

Seven bit her lip and nodded.

"Okay. While we're walking, let's play a game. I'll throw things in your path. Instead of stepping over them, use one of your powers. The faster you call on them, the faster we'll get to the tunnel in Zimbabwe."

"I don't think you understand. We don't have

a lot of time. If we wait too long, people could die."

Cam nodded gravely. "Yes. And if you don't do this, you will die, and then lots of people will die. This is important, Seven."

No pressure. Seven gulped. "Okay. I better learn fast then, huh?" she said with a weak smile.

"I'll help! I love to throw things in Seven's way," Haran said cheerfully.

She glanced at the horizon behind them. There was no cloud. As she spun in a slow circle, she could see no cloud anywhere. For the moment, at least, they were safe. "Okay. Let's all have fun throwing things at Seven. Ready?"

She spent the next hour tripping over sticks that appeared in her path out of nowhere, rocks thrown under her feet, and sometimes Cam, who liked to shove her when she got too comfortable. Haran tried, but she was still bigger than him. For most of that hour, she was either on her hands and knees, or pitching head first before Cam caught her.

It was a painful hour.

But then she got annoyed. And she had

realized being angry or annoyed woke her banshee half faster than anything else. As they wore into the second hour, she blasted sticks with her heat before they could even hit the ground. She tripped but flew, instead of fell. She screamed a few times, but the sound waves nearly deafened Haran and Cam both, besides blowing holes in the grasses before them.

It wasn't as hot in Zimbabwe as it was Egypt, but it wasn't anywhere near as cool as Ireland. The sun burned Seven's fair skin and she wished she would have thought to bring sun block. Far off on the horizon, she could see the city rising from the savannah, but for now they were surrounded by grass and trees. Some were palm trees-which she'd seen in pictures. Others were long and spindly trees that looked almost petrified. Maybe because of lack of water. She would have killed for a tour guide right about then.

Then there were the mountains. Lots of mountains. And huge outcroppings of rock rising from the earth.

And animals! There were animals wandering

in the distance—giraffes, and a herd of elephants. They passed zebras grazing almost within arms' reach of them, and only a few raised their heads to watch the three human-like creatures walk by. Apparently, only animals from Ireland were afraid of banshees. Haran was so excited he forgot to throw things for her, squealing when they heard a lion roar in the distance. Seven wasn't nearly as amused. It would be just her luck to make it this far and be killed by something not even magical.

"I pictured Africa as, like, having little villages with grass huts and stuff," Haran said, looking around with eyes so wide, Seven worried they'd fall out of his head.

"Me too. Maybe we're too close to the city for that?" She glanced at Cam, but he shrugged.

"I've lived in Atlantis my whole life."

She wanted to ask what it was like, being surrounded by magical creatures all the time. Having people of your own kind. She wondered what Atlantis looked like. She'd seen pictures on SplashSpace and knew it was an underwater city, protected by a bubble that made it so no one from the outside world could find it. But the little details that she couldn't see in a picture—those were the things she wanted to know.

But she knew what her mother had done, when she'd taken one of her souls there to try to protect him. She'd thought he was threatened and screamed and nearly blew the place up, or so Seven had heard. She knew what people thought of banshees in Atlantis—and half-breed banshees are worse. They were dangerous and evil.

Seven was dangerous. But she wasn't evil.

She realized her head was hanging like a dejected, kicked puppy, and she raised her chin defiantly. She wasn't in Atlantis. No one could see her defiance. But it still made her feel better. Until she caught sight of the horizon. A black cloud formed—far off, but still there. She thought of all the bad words her dad had forbidden her to say, and stifled the urge to say any of them. Which made her very proud of herself.

"Cam, tell me about the gates. Why are they closing them?" she asked to distract herself, to hide her fear from Haran. To do some research so she'd understand better what she was facing.

Her dad would be pleased. He was always telling her to do as much research beforehand as possible—except he was usually talking about science fair projects and math tests.

Cam sighed, running a hand over his face. "There's this guy named Phoibos. He wants to get rid of all the hybrids. He believes they're tainting Atlantis. To do that, he's forcing them out and closing the gates with magical powers so that only he or his minions can open them."

"Then . . . why did the seer tell the Egyptian guardian demons that I could help?"

Cam shrugged. "She knows something we don't, apparently."

"Helpful, Cam. Very helpful," she said, teasing, because she could tell the unknown frightened him.

They'd been walking for some time when Seven could hear a roar that was definitely not animal-made. It seemed to be coming from all around them, and she turned in a slow circle but couldn't see anything that would make that kind of noise.

"It's a waterfall," Cam said. "Sounds like a

pretty big one."

Seven's brain clicked, and her eyes lit up. "Oh! I know! It's Victoria Falls—the biggest waterfall in the world. I mean, it's not as wide or as high as some of the others, but its combined height times width makes it the biggest. It's in Zimbabwe! We must be close to the next tunnel!"

"The tunnel is in the abandoned mines. They're surrounded by an outcropping of rock," Cam said.

Seven raised an eyebrow, looking around them. *They* were surrounded by outcroppings of rock. "Great. No problem. We'll just pick one and hope we find it."

"Africa is pretty," Haran said, completely oblivious to Death's return or Cam and Seven's stress.

Seven smiled. "Yeah it is."

"What is that animal? I've never seen that in my books." Haran pointed and Seven raised her hand, squinting to see into the sun. In the distance was a weird-looking dog thing, or at least that's what Seven thought at first.

But on closer inspection, it was not a dog. It

had a lizard-like tail, furry spikes on its long back, and short legs. Seven didn't realize the thing was a demon until she saw the head—no skin or fur, just a skull, with the typical red, glowing eyes of a demon. And a long, long forked tongue, like a snake. It raced through the tall grasses, straight toward them.

"Get behind me!" Seven yelled, shoving Haran and Cam both behind her before either of them could react.

"I'm an Atlantian guard, Seven. I think I can take care of—" But he stopped as the thing skidded to a halt in front of them. "What is that?" he whispered.

And then it bounced away, looking over its shoulder at them.

"I know what it is," Haran said, peeking fearlessly around the arm Seven was unsuccessfully using to hold him back. "I did a report on it for our African continent week."

Seven didn't risk looking back at him. "I think it wants us to follow it. Maybe it's another demon sent from the seer to guide us?" It occurred to her then to wonder why the seer only sent demons to help her. Didn't the woman have any not-evil friends?

She could feel Haran shaking his head, because his whole small body shook with it. Apparently, he was seriously against this. "It's an Abiku. A West African demon that tempts children away from home and then eats them. We should *not* follow it."

"It's either follow that one or get attacked by this one," Cam yelled. Seven spun, her arms still out, to see another one racing toward them through the grass. As soon as their backs were turned, she could hear the first one coming again.

"Holy crap!" Seven gasped as a third one, and then a fourth, appeared on both sides. They were surrounded.

"Seven, get them!"

Seven nodded, letting loose a scream that tore the grass in front of her. The creature was flipped end over end, but it didn't burst into a thousand pieces like she'd been expecting. She didn't have time to think on it though. She screamed while she whirled in a circle, careful to keep Haran and Cam behind her. The demons were knocked backward, all of them, but none of them died or exploded or anything.

"Haran! In your report, how do you kill these things?" she gasped, her throat aching.

"Umm . . . I can't . . ."

"Haran!"

"Iron! They're allergic to iron!"

Seven slapped a hand to her forehead. "We don't have any iron, Haran!"

Cam unsheathed the swords Seven hadn't even noticed he was carrying. "I will fight them."

"Are those iron?" Seven asked hopefully. The creatures were back on their short little legs and already coming after them again.

"They're steel," Cam said, sounding offended.

That didn't help Seven at all. "Is steel iron?" she yelled, considering whether or not to risk a grass fire just to try to kill these things with her lasers. It seemed too dangerous, so instead she started to sing. Her ghosts rose in front of her, around her, protecting her. They had weapons this time, and even though they were made of the same transparent ghostly-ness as her army, when one sliced into the Abiku, it was definitely solid enough to do some damage.

But not enough.

"It's not stopping them. They're cutting right through the ghosts. We've gotta figure out something else," Seven panted.

"Might I suggest running?" Haran yelped, nearly climbing up Seven's arm.

"They're surrounding us. We have nowhere to run."

Cam leaped in front of them, swinging his sword heroically. The Abiku grabbed it with its long forked tongue and dragged it back to its mouth, chomping it in two. "Apparently Atlantian steel isn't iron," he gasped, stumbling back to Seven's side.

"Salt!" Haran dropped his pack to the ground and started rummaging through it. Seven stared at him—clearly her little brother had lost his mind.

"Haran! Now is not a good time to eat!" she shrieked, shaking the air around them. He paused only long enough to give her a withering glare, and went back to digging.

Seven screamed again, knocking them back,

but they were faster to get up this time. They were a bloody mess from her ghosts' attack, but it didn't seem to slow them much. Ghost weapons must not be made of iron, either. "Okay, maybe they just want someone to pet them. I mean, even demon creatures need love, right?" Seven asked as they slowly walked, back to back, in a circle around Haran.

"Salt!" he yelled, jumping up triumphantly with a packet of salt in his hands. "Seven, when I say scream, scream!" Seven gaped at him, but what choice did they have? The demon creatures were about to eat them and fight over their bones.

Haran ran in front of her, backing up several steps so he wasn't in her direct path, and ripped the salt packet open, tipping it sideways. "Scream!" he dumped the salt and dove out of the way, covering his ears. Seven screamed and the salt flew away from her, coasting on the sound waves, until Seven couldn't see it anymore.

"Why did I do that, Haran?" she gasped.

He grabbed her arm, jerking her toward the next Abiku. "Do it again!" he said, sprinkling the salt and Seven, completely bewildered, did it again. She was not used to being bossed around by her brother, but he was pretty adamant.

"Look! The creatures do not react well to the salt!" Cam crowed. Seven risked a glance over her shoulder as Haran tugged her on toward the next one, which was dangerously close now. The first one was bubbling and oozing in a hundred different places—everywhere that the grains of salt had landed on it.

"It kills them! Do the next one! Hurry, Sev!" Haran leaned away, sprinkling the salt, and Seven screamed again. Her throat felt like someone had attacked the inside with a pitchfork.

Cam hit her from behind and they tumbled through the grass. The fourth one had gotten to them before she could get to it. Haran crawled backward on hands and feet like a crab as Seven struggled to get to her knees. The thing stalked him, snorting, its long tongue flicking dangerously.

Seven couldn't scream without hurting Haran. She reached for her laser eyes, deciding a grass fire was worth the risk. Haran jerked his arm up just as the thing lunged for him, and the remainder of salt flew into its face. It shrieked, giving even Seven a run for her money, and stumbled backward, shaking its long, skull-like head back and forth desperately. It crashed to the ground, oozing, and lay still. All around them, the Abikus were dead.

CHAPTER TEN:
HELLO, DEATH

The smell of rapidly decaying Abikus was horrific. It was the smell of road kill baking in the sun. Seven gagged and covered her nose. Haran's face was positively green as he scrambled away from it to Seven's side. "Are you okay?" she asked him.

He nodded quickly. "Cam?" she breathed.

"I'm fine."

"Ghosts? Thank you. I think they're dead." Seven gagged. Her ghosts raised their hands in farewell and were gone, almost like they were in a hurry to get away from the smell as well. Haran leaned against her shoulder and she slumped back against Cam. "Well that was . . . awful."

"But we survived," Cam said optimistically.

"Thanks to Haran. You're a hero." She ruffled his hair.

"It wouldn't have worked without your scream," he said, his little voice exhausted.

"My scream was worthless. How am I supposed to defeat a Kraken if I can't even defeat Phoibos's minions?"

Cam patted her on the shoulder and then pushed her to her feet. "I can't stand the smell any longer." Haran followed them as they picked their way through the dead, still-bubbling bodies.

"Lady Kraken is big, but she is slow. You are small and fast. And you will not face her alone, Seven," Cam said.

Seven smiled up at him, grateful for Cam's presence even if his sword had been as useless as any of her powers. "Look at that over there—is it an old mine or something?"

Cam squinted and Haran skipped ahead to check it out. Sure, he could skip. He hadn't been tripping and falling all day long. His energy wasn't completely gone. "I think there is a mine over there, Sev! Come check it out!"

Seven sighed. "Children." But she lengthened

her stride and hurried after him, climbing the rocky hill until she stood panting at his side. Cam climbed easily next to her, and she had the distinct urge to kick him. No matter how nice he was. She put her hands on her knees and sucked in deep breaths before standing up to see what Haran thought was so cool.

And saw Death.

"Haran—get back!" Seven jumped in front of him. She didn't know what, exactly, she would do; it wasn't like she had the power to stop Death. But she'd been watching so carefully. She'd kept him in the distance, just a dark cloud on the horizon. How had he found Haran so quickly?

Haran blinked at her and moved backward. "What's wrong?"

Seven opened her mouth. How did you explain to someone that they were about to die? She could cry for him, which was what she'd been born to do. But there was a part of her that was furious. She did not want Death to take her brother. She hadn't dragged him all over the world just to lose him now. Straightening her spine, she prepared to give Death a very firm talking to.

He wasn't there.

"Seven?" Haran asked slowly, watching her like she'd lost her mind.

Death wasn't here for him. Death was here for someone else.

"Someone's in trouble. Haran…" She spun on him, gripping his shoulders. "You can n*ot* follow me. Death is here and if he sees you, he might take you. Stay here until I come back. Promise?"

"Yeah." He nodded, meeting her eyes. "Yeah, I'll stay here."

"Good. Cam? Stay here with him. If anything happens—" But what could Cam do? He couldn't even *see* Death, let alone fight him. "Just protect my brother. Please?"

Cam, too, nodded his agreement.

Seven spun away, racing over the rocks, leaping into the air and coasting on the light breeze. It was dangerous, using her banshee half so much. The temptation to not return to her human half was stronger every time. And would it be so bad if she were to stay a banshee?

She came over the rise and fell out of the air. There was a mine shaft, and at the very end of it, she could just see a very, very pink lake, waters swirling eagerly. She'd never seen a pink lake before. Never even heard of one, in fact. "That's . . . very strange."

But she wasn't here to look for a lake. She twirled in circles, looking for Death. She finally caught sight of his shadow, stopped a few feet from something immobile. Seven crept closer, trying to see past him, when a figure stood up directly across from Death. The boy was carrying someone, but it wasn't human—although Seven was pretty sure it was a girl of whatever species it was. And there was another creature with him, but this one was up on his feet, also holding someone, not human. The boy walked forward, unmindful of Death, and smashed into . . . something Seven couldn't see. Electrical sparks shot up around him. He turned to his companion and said something, laid the girl down he was carrying, and walked forward through what Seven decided was a magical wall of some sort. Sparks flew around him, but the wall let him through.

Seven jerked back as he came closer, stumbled on a rock and landed on her butt. The boy ignored her, pacing in and out through the wall, sparks and bits of flame erupting around him each time. So the wall didn't keep humans out, apparently.

But it did seem to keep Death out. He stood staring at it, red eyes glowing dangerously but unable to get through.

She scrambled to her feet and ran after the boy. "Hey! Hey you!" He spun, dark hair still standing on end from walking through the invisible wall. "What are you doing?" she asked, landing in front of him. Between him and Death, who still stood, completely baffled.

"My friends are on the other side. If they can't get to the water, they'll die." the boy answered. Seven looked past Death. The creature she'd seen carrying one of the others raced toward the wall, slammed into it, and bounced back.

"What is he?" she asked. Maybe it only blocked certain magical creatures?

"He's a kelpie. On the ground—those are all Naiads."

Seven followed the boy over, glancing nervously at Death, but he seemed to have a one track mind and ignored her completely. Which was convenient. What exactly did one say when one was trying to thwart the very creature one was born to help?

She reached a hand out, feeling the spark of electrical current run through her. Not solid. Like a force field or something. But it kept her out, too.

It kept her out. But it wouldn't keep her scream out. "Get back," she said quietly.

The boy glanced at her from where he stood half-through the wall. "What?"

"Get back. I think I can get through it." Mustering her courage, she turned to Death. "You too. You need to get out of the way." She could feel his eyes on her, but she refused to meet his gaze. They'd met many times, as she'd handed her souls off to him. He wasn't evil. He wasn't mean. He was a guide into the afterlife. And she'd rather not blow him to pieces. He slid backward, and she wondered, not for the first time, if he had feet.

The boy, too, had backed away. She hurried over to him, speaking quickly but keeping her voice low. "We'll have to race Death. As soon as the wall is gone, you grab your friends and get them to the water. Do you understand?"

His brown eyes widened. "What are you?"

"I'm a banshee. Cover your ears." She turned and jogged away, back toward the wall. It was overwhelming, trying to scream when Death stood so near, watching silently. Her first attempt sounded almost human—weak and terrified. The wall sparked but it didn't blow up. She had to dig down deep, she had to beg her banshee half to rise and conquer her own fear.

And then she screamed.

The wall shattered into a million shards of energy. She felt it burn her skin in a thousand tiny spots, but the boy and the other creature were already running forward, right through the deluge. So she followed him, even though she could barely see through all the sparks still falling through the air. She grabbed one of the naiads under the arms and leaped into the air.

Seven felt Death brush her foot as they flew toward the water, but he didn't catch her. Or the girl she carried. Naiad? She'd never seen one, but she'd heard rumors. As she dove down toward the water and her vision finally cleared, she saw that her first guess had been right. This girl was definitely not human. She had mother of pearl skin, blushing in faded blues, pinks, and greens. Her eyes, one blue and one green, still glowed faintly through half-closed eyelids. Limp green hair hung down her scaly back in tangled knots.

Seven dropped her into the water, watching in fascination as the pink waves splashed around them. "Are there more?" she asked, watching the naiad sink below the surface, out of sight. The boy and a creature which looked an awful lot like a horse covered in blue seaweed helped the other two naiads into the pink pool. The water began to bubble and turn blue.

"No." The boy shook his head, brushing dark brown hair out of his eyes. "No, that's it. I don't—I—Thank you. Thank you for breaking the wall. I'm Adam."

"I'm Seven." She smiled. "And no problem." Her eyes scanned the rocks, looking for Death. But he was gone. "My brother might be in trouble. I'm sorry to leave you, I hope you're okay. I've gotta go!" she whirled and jumped into the air, felt her skin lighten and her weight fade, as she shot back toward Haran.

"Please don't be dead."

He wasn't dead. Instead, Haran waited for her at the mouth of the mine. "How did you do that?"

"You're alive!" she squealed, landing next to him and throwing her arms around him. "I was afraid Death left us and came for you."

"Nope." It would be okay. Everything would be okay. "And again I ask, how did you do that? That was a magical wall. The guardian demons said that only Phoibos and his minions could undo that kind of magic." Haran waved his arms all over like he wasn't quite sure where to point.

"I don't know."

Cam spoke up. "There are only seven half-breed banshees to ever live. Maybe you have magic Phoibos is unprepared for. Maybe that's why the seer said you had to be the one to defeat Lady Kraken—not because you're the only one who can kill *her*, but because you're the only one who can break open the gate behind her."

"Wow. My sister is all famous and stuff." Haran snickered.

"Speaking of your sister . . . didn't I tell you to not follow me?"

"I was worried!" Haran said.

"He wanted to see you blow stuff up," Cam said, grinning.

"Haran!" she swiped at him and he yelped, dancing backward away from her half-hearted attempt to smack him.

And into the hands of Death.

His face paled as Death reached out, icy hands grasping Haran's soul. "No!" Seven screamed.

Death tumbled backward, his grip loosening. Haran fell forward, stumbling into Seven's arms. She hadn't meant to attack Death—it had been instinct. But he was still struggling to get to his feet and she wasn't one to waste an opportunity. She grabbed Haran, holding him tight against her, and leaped into the sky. "Cam! Death is here—I have to go! I have to get Haran to the Fountain of Youth!"

Below her, Cam's eyes widened in shock and he nodded quickly. "The tunnel is across the rocks—in the cave. Hurry, Seven! I will meet you in Atlantis!"

Seven didn't reply. Death was upright, coming after her, because he could fly too, and probably faster than she could. She tightened her grip on Haran and spun through the currents, straight through like a bullet as she screamed, blowing anything in their way into broken bits of nothing.

She saw the cave as Death reached for her ankle. She and Haran could both die here, she knew. If Death caught her, he might take her soul as punishment for trying to save her brother. And then Haran would have no one to protect him. She dropped out of the sky, landed hard, and watched as Death shot past them. He skidded in mid-air, trying to turn around. Seven leaped into the air again and ducked underneath him.

She roared into the cave, praying with

everything she had that there were no bad guys blocking this one. She landed hard, felt the rocks rain on her head, and still holding her brother, dragged him around the cave until she found the marks. Death appeared in the doorway, his red eyes glowing angrily in his hood. *"Seven, it is his time."*

"No. No it isn't. I'm sorry," she sobbed. "I'm sorry, but you can't take him," she said as she stumbled backward. Into the wall—but the wall opened and she and Haran fell through.

They were on a platform. Behind them were slides—like the slippery slides at the playground near her home in Ireland, but a gazillion feet long and winding down at a gentle slope through the tunnel. They got to slide all the way to Japan? Haran would love that.

Except Haran wasn't moving.

She laid her brother on the platform and knelt next to him. "Haran?" she cried, leaning close to his chest. His heart still beat, and she could feel his breath on her hair, but his eyes wouldn't open.

The Fountain. The Fountain could heal him.

It would save him, and then she'd forget about Atlantis and take him home. They'd go back to Ireland and she'd never let him out of her sight again and Death would never find him. Yes. That's what would happen. She scooped him up under the arms and dragged him to the slide. Positioning him in front of her, she sat behind him and pushed off.

They slid through the tunnel. She felt the tears soak her cheeks as she imagined how Haran would have loved this. He would have been screaming "wheeeeee!" with his hands in the air, maybe trying to stop mid-slide and jumping to the one next to him. He would flip over and try sliding on his stomach, lay back and take a nap on his back. And he'd complain that he was hungry, because it had been hours and hours since they'd eaten.

Seven held him tighter against her chest and sobbed. "Hang on, Haran. Just hang on a little longer. We're almost there." The wind brushed the tears off her cheeks like gentle fingers, so that they dampened her curls against her temples. What if she didn't make it in time? How would she possibly know how to exist without him? Haran was her best friend. In a life where she was so different from everyone else, where she had so many secrets that no one would understand, he was the bright light holding her to humanity. Banshees were sad. They spent their lives mourning the deaths of those in their care. But with Haran, Seven hadn't ever had time to be sad. She'd laughed and played and had a childhood and happy memories.

"Just hang on."

She could feel him breathing. It was slow and shallow, but they were breaths. She could feel his weak heart beat under her hands and knew that Death may have had a grip on his soul, but dang it, so did she. And just this once, she had to be stronger than Death. Nothing else mattered.

She fell asleep. On a slippery slide. She didn't know how it happened but the winding twists and gentle slope somehow put her to sleep. She didn't wake until they thumped into the wall at the bottom. "Oh!" she gasped, her eyes flying open.

Haran stirred, moaning. "Seven?" he asked weakly. His eyes fluttered, revealing the dark, dark circles hidden beneath his thick lashes. He was so pale.

"I'm here, Haran. Just stay with me. We're almost there."

She looked up at the ladder leading to the doorway on the surface. How was she supposed to carry him up? She knew firemen could do it, but she didn't have their strength.

You're a banshee, Seven.

She nearly smacked herself in the forehead. She could fly him up there. One day, this banshee thing would be second nature, and then she wouldn't have dilemmas like whether to kick herself or roll her eyes at her own stupidity. She couldn't wait for that day.

Seven clutched him tight again and flew up, pushing the lever so the doorway swung open. She'd just settled Haran on the ground when she dropped from the air like a rock with arms and legs. She hit the side of the opening and tumbled back down into the tunnel, landing hard on the ground. The room spun and black splotches appeared in front of her, like mini-Akies flying around her head. Groaning, she sat up. What in the world was that?

She rubbed the back of her head where she could feel a goose egg already forming, and mentally ran through the list of bad words her dad didn't let her say. It helped, so she climbed to her feet and leaped into the air.

And fell back to earth. "Oof!" she grunted as her legs crumpled beneath her.

She couldn't fly.

The weightlessness she usually felt when she tried to fly wasn't there. She closed her eyes, searching her heart for her banshee half. She could feel it, but it was as if it was locked away from her. She couldn't get to it.

Scrambling up the ladder, she turned away from Haran and tried to scream. It was the easiest of all her powers, it came the most naturally. But this time, it was just a regular, boring old scared-girl scream. Nothing quaked or swayed or tumbled away from her, let alone blew up. "No. no, no, no, no, no!" Seven muttered, closing her eyes tight and trying to find the warmth for her eyes. But it was a half-hearted attempt. Deep down, she knew she wouldn't be able to. And deep down, she was right. The warmth was locked away with the rest of her banshee half.

Somehow, she'd lost her magic.

CHAPTER ELEVEN: GIANT CHICKENS AND LAVA ROCK

Okay. It's okay." Seven jumped around in a tight circle, shaking her hands like she'd just had a good run at whatever sport normal people played. "I just have to get Haran to the Fountain and then we can go home. I don't need my magic." Nodding to agree with herself, she hurried over to Haran, scooping him up and muttering under her breath about the fact that he was nearly as big as she was.

She hoped it wasn't a large island.

She'd already noticed Death looming on the horizon. He was tracking them much more quickly than before, probably because of his hold on Haran's soul. She didn't have a lot of time.

Pausing to catch her breath, she leaned Haran against her and let her arms drop, trying to get the feeling back in her hands.

She'd always heard that Japan was green and beautiful. This island, however, was black and sharp. A volcano rose at the far end, smoke wafting from the mouth. Blackened trees rose in gnarled tangles around her, and the ground was petrified lava under her feet. She couldn't remember if anyone had thought to mention to her that the Fountain of Youth was on an island with an active volcano. If she could fly, it wouldn't have been such a big deal. But she could not fly, and she could not even run and carry Haran at the same time. All she could do was pray really hard that the volcano didn't decide to erupt while they were there.

Knowing her luck, it probably would.

She wandered, retraced her steps, got lost, and fell several times. The petrified lava was *sharp*, and her knees were a bloody mess. She wanted to lay Haran down so she could move faster, but she didn't dare leave him. Not with the big, black cloud on the horizon, coming closer every second. Not when she couldn't see very far in any direction because of the swells and ebbs of the petrified lava and the rising hills all around them.

She stopped for the eight hundredth time and resisted the urge to cry. She couldn't be lost right now! Gritting her teeth with determination, she balanced Haran against her shoulder. "Okay. If I were a legendary Fountain of Youth, where would I be...?" She scanned the area all around them, looking for any sign of water at all. The only trace was the ocean in the distance, and that wasn't what she was looking for.

"The most unlikely place for it would be at the base of the volcano. And since everything in this magical life of mine is where it shouldn't be, that must be where it is." Nodding to agree with herself once again, because there was no one else to do it, she looped her little brother's arm over her shoulder again and stumbled forward, slowly, one step at a time. But with determination. Her back ached, her arms ached. She was tired and hungry and thirsty. And she was human.

And her human self found the Fountain.

They came up the side of a hill and there it

stood, only twenty feet away. She could see that the water was different, sort of swirly and sparkly as it bubbled out of the volcano like a spring. She checked on Death, breathing a silent sigh of relief that he was still far enough away, and started forward again.

Fire erupted in front of her.

At first, her startled brain thought it was the volcano. But it was a horizontal burst of fire, like when she shot from her laser eyes. She scrambled backward out of the way, dragging Haran with her. Instead of the heat she was expecting, though, it was a burst of cool air, and despite the fact that her stray curl got caught in the wave of fire, it didn't burn, it sort of froze—like liquid ice. *Odd.*

When it seemed the blasting was done, she ever so cautiously peeked her head around the black lava to see where it had come from.

A giant chicken stood there, glaring at her.

She jerked her head back, sucking in a breath. A chicken? Why did it have to be a chicken? She'd been afraid of chickens since she was little and the mean neighbors had locked her in their chicken coop. Now there was a giant, ice-breathing chicken waiting to turn the tables and roast *her,* instead of the other way around. Could things get any less fun?

She felt it coming closer, the ground shaking with every step of its big feet. Her desperate eyes found the Fountain. She'd been right, it was at the base of the volcano. Right where it shouldn't be, like the rest of her crazy life. So close, but so impossibly far away. "Haran, I'm going to lay you down right here," she whispered, sliding his arm over her head and lowering him to the ground. "Don't let Death find you, and don't let the giant chicken step on you. I'll be right back." She dropped the backpacks from her other shoulder and dug through one to find an empty water bottle. Good thing their dad had taught them not to litter, or she wouldn't have had one handy.

She darted out from behind her hill, racing toward the Fountain with her water bottle clutched tightly in her hand. The chicken squawked. The sound reverberated through the lava, causing it to crumble and break. The chunks rained down on her head. She threw her hands up to protect herself and shrieked back at the chicken.

Nothing happened.

Nothing except that the chicken got angrier. It blew the cold fire out of his beak as it squawked. Seven dove backward as the flames blew over her, not burning, but cold. Cold fire. How did that make any sense?

It didn't, but she didn't have time to care. It was already racing toward her, determined, it seemed, to keep her away from the Fountain. She scrambled to her feet and raced sideways, leading it away from Haran, but further from the Fountain. The angry chicken followed, blowing the cold fire at her whenever it got close enough. She spent more time diving out of the way than she did actually running, and the big bird caught up to her before she'd gotten very far. She leaped into the sky, forgetting momentarily that she couldn't fly. She tumbled back to the ground, landing hard on her elbows and stomach. By now she was a mass of cuts and bruises from the sharp lava rock, and no closer to the Fountain than she was before. Trying to be a banshee would get her killed.

She leaped up and sprinted away, dodging around creases in the lava when the fire nearly hit her. As she ran, she heard a whisper, and then a voice. Her dad's voice. His words—something he'd told her a thousand times.

You're more than a banshee, Seven. You're my little girl.

His little girl. His human little girl. She'd embraced her banshee half these past few days, so much that she'd nearly forgotten her human half. But her banshee half wasn't here, and her human half was, and she needed to use it.

"Thanks, Dad," she murmured.

She had to lead the chicken away from Haran and away from the Fountain, instead of running back and forth in front of them, waiting for her scream to miraculously make an appearance. With at least a half a plan in mind, she made a sharp turn and sprinted toward the ocean. Toward Death, who she could almost see now in his cloud. She didn't have much time. The chicken squawked again and Seven dove and rolled sideways. On this side of the island, there was grass and trees. And the ocean. She wondered how chickens felt about water.

She raced out to the beach, grateful for the soft sand when she had to fall to the side to avoid more fire. "Hey, you stupid chicken! Come get me!" She leaped to her feet and ran into the water, waving her arms and screaming. The chicken gave an enraged squawk and pounded after her, its giant feet making the waves rock higher and harder. They nearly knocked Seven over in their fury.

Apparently it had had enough of trying to roast her with its cold fire and now wanted to peck her to death. But unlike the chickens at home, this beak could cut her in half with one hit.

She'd like to avoid that.

It waddled onto the beach and lunged, but she was too far away. It seemed to really want to keep its feet out of the water. Instead it got a beakful of ocean salt and seaweed. It jerked its head up, sputtering and angrier than before. It opened its beak to blow fire at her again, but choked on the water instead. As it sat, hacking and coughing, Seven sprinted out of the water and ran for all she was worth back to the Fountain.

She could tell when the chicken realized she was gone because she could feel its footsteps pounding behind her, shaking the petrified lava under her feet. But she was too far ahead now, and chickens weren't the smartest animals in the world. It got lost, which Seven could also tell because of the footsteps—they got further away until the ground didn't shake, and then they were closer and knocking Seven off her feet, and then they were gone again. She allowed herself one triumphant grin before she skidded around the corner and found the Fountain.

Death's cloud was gone. Which meant he was here, somewhere. Seven sprinted across the lava, uncorking the water bottle she still held clutched in her hand. It was dented and battered, but thankfully still in one piece. Without hesitating, she thrust it into the water, bouncing impatiently on her toes until it was nearly full, and then raced to Haran. She had a brief moment of wanting to sob with absolute relief that he still lay where she'd left him, and that she could still see his chest rise and fall, but there was no time or energy for sobbing. She fell to her knees, ignoring the pain when the rocks dug into her skin, and held the water up to Haran's lips.

Death walked around the corner.

She raised wide, frightened eyes to his. "Please. Please don't take him."

"It is not a Banshee's place to hold souls here when they're meant to move on."

"I—I know." She was sobbing because he kept coming closer and closer and she didn't dare take her eyes from him. "I know, but he's my brother. He's my best friend. Please—"

Death stopped and watched her for several long seconds. *"You have had a heart-breaking childhood. You have faced it with bravery."*

She swallowed, hiccupping twice, confused. "Thank you," she whispered.

"It isn't a chicken. It's a Japanese demon called a Basan." Haran's weak voice scared Seven so much she nearly dropped the water bottle.

"Haran!" she squealed, setting the water aside and throwing her arms around him. He coughed and his eyes drifted closed. "Wait—wait!" She looked up at Death but he hadn't moved. "What's wrong? I gave you the water!"

"I'm just . . . tired."

"Drink some more. It will help."

Death's red eyes dimmed, reminding her distinctly of Akie when he was sad. *"Many of the gates to Atlantis have been closed, which cuts off the magic between our world and theirs."* His robe-hidden arm swept to the side where Seven was startled to see a distinctive gate—not like the doorways to the tunnels. But there was no light or magic or anything. It looked . . . dead. *"This gate usually keeps the Fountain's magic strong and healthy. But with the gate closed, the Fountain's magic isn't strong enough to save him for long."*

"But—but we came all this way! I fought the chicken! I don't—"

"Basan," Haran said tiredly, struggling to sit up.

She met Death's eyes, holding his gaze for several long, long seconds. "Have I lost him, then?"

He didn't blink, didn't answer. Just continued to stare at her. She scrubbed at her tears and brushed Haran's hair away from his forehead.

Then Death nodded once. *"Take him to Atlantis and open the gate. Near the Collective of power in Atlantis, the water will resume its strength and he will live. But you don't have long, banshee Seven."*

Seven nodded so hard her neck popped several times. "Okay. Okay, we can do that. Okay. Thank you. Thank you so much."

He slowly backed away and was gone. Seven raced back over to the Fountain and filled up her water bottle, screwing the lid on tight. Then she shoved everything into their bags and threw both bags over her shoulder.

"Ready?" she asked breathlessly. They'd been given time, but not much. She could see Haran still fighting for his life, and even Death couldn't give him another chance if they didn't hurry.

Haran nodded, pushing himself away from the lava he'd been leaning against. Seven took his hand and pulled him to his feet, looping his arm around her neck like before. It was much, much easier making their way back across the petrified plains when she wasn't lost and carrying a completely unconscious Haran, although he was leaning most of his weight on her. They had to stop several times so he could rest, as sweat beaded on his forehead and his little arms shook. Her usually very talkative brother didn't speak at all, as if saving all his strength to make it to the tunnel. And what if they had to walk all the way to Atlantis? They'd left the scooters in the tunnel on the way to Zimbabwe. Seven's powers had gone who-knew-where. What if there wasn't a convenient slippery slide to Atlantis?

She couldn't think about that now. She had to focus on putting one foot in front of the other. *Just get to the tunnel. One step at a time, sweetie.* Her dad's voice again. A wave of homesickness hit her so hard she nearly buckled under Haran's weight. But no, she could be strong. She was strong because she was her mother's daughter—and her father's daughter. She was half-banshee and half-human and wholly Seven.

They made it to the tunnel that would take them back to Zimbabwe, and from there, to Atlantis. A thrill of nerves ran through her at the thought of seeing the legendary city in person and knowing a mighty sea creature waited there to eat her. Or whatever Krakens did. "Okay. Rest right here for a sec. Let me just get the tunnel open . . ." Seven leaned Haran on the most comfortable looking bit of lava she could find and held her hand to the doorway.

Nothing happened.

"What in the world?" She bent down, searching for a lever or a button or something, but there was nothing except the signs that showed her where the doorway was. "I think this one is broken. We'll have to find another one."

Haran looked like he might cry, but her little brother was braver than she was. He nodded and struggled to his feet. Again they made slow progress through the waves of petrified lava, being careful not to trip. Seven's knees couldn't lose any more skin. Her hands, either.

She found two more tunnels. Neither of them would open. Would they have to swim to the mainland? Haran would never make it. "Something's blocking them. Like in Egypt. Something is keeping them from opening." She blinked. A bad guy in Egypt had held the key— and Seven had only run into one bad guy on all her travels around this stupid island.

"It's the chicken."

"Basan," Haran wheezed.

"Haran…" She leaned down so they were face to face. "I have to go kill the Basan. It must hold the key to the doorway." *Lady Kraken must have sent it to stop me. That, or I've lost my magic so the tunnels won't open for me and we're stuck here forever.* "Wait here for me."

"You—you don't have any—any magic Because—because of the Basan. He's stealing your magic."

"It's okay. Dad taught me a thing or two." She forced a bright smile. "I got this. Just wait here for me."

CHAPTER TWELVE:
TWO HALVES
MAKE A SEVEN

Seven's dad had always told her, "Have a plan, Seven. You can't go wrong with a plan." Of course, he was usually talking about how to tackle her homework or beat him at chess, but it sounded like good advice now. She didn't have her powers. She had started to expect that she could scream at something and it would go away, but this journey seemed bent on teaching her first that she was a banshee, then it seemed to change its mind and decided to teach her that she was a human.

Okay then.

She racked her brain, trying to remember everything she knew about chickens. She knew people thought they were dumb but they were actually sort of smart. She knew this one, at least, didn't like the ocean. She knew its fire wouldn't burn her, but it was cold and it hurt. She knew it was a demon. And that it really, really didn't like her.

Did it hate her enough to run into a volcano?

It was possible, but how would she *not* run into the volcano? She discarded that idea. She could pretend to be a chick and when it brought her food . . . what? She had no weapons. She raced around the corner and found herself right above the chicken. It was nesting, blue fire snapping in and out of its mouth as it snored. She watched it, studying the area around her, and she noticed something she hadn't in the sprinting all over—rats. Lots and lots of rats. Her skin crawled. Awesome. Rats and chickens and her, all stuck together on an island. She'd had the idea before and it hit her again—could life get any more fun?

She thought not.

They were near the base of the volcano, and it rumbled dangerously, shards of mountain crashing around her. She slipped and nearly went over the edge, catching herself just in time on the jagged edge of lava rock. She cursed and tugged herself up, crawling back away from the edge so she wouldn't fall off again. Forgetting the Basan for a second, she studied the volcano. Smoke poured from the opening and the ground trembled under her feet. She didn't know much about volcanoes, but instinct told her that the thing was about to erupt. And when it did, the Basan would be the least of her worries. She bit her lip, staring at the volcano, the rats, the chicken, and she could not think of one single plan.

Her dad would be so disappointed.

The boulder she leaned against wobbled dangerously, its sharp edges cutting into the rock beneath it. Every time the volcano acted up a little, it rolled forward. One push, and she could shove it over the edge. Which was a great plan, if the chicken was a little closer.

So make it come closer, Seven.

Her dad's voice echoed in her head. She knew he couldn't actually talk to her via mental telepathy, or she would have pestered him for help during math tests, but hearing him was still a comfort.

And he was a genius.

She had to make that chicken mad and bring it closer.

She scampered around her little outcropping, looking for a way down that could also be a quick way up. Luckily, because the rocks were so roily and jagged, they had lots of handholds and footholds—painful handholds and footholds, but they were there.

"Okay, Dad. I've got a plan. Let's hope I don't get pecked to death trying to carry it out."

She skidded down the side of her outcropping, making sure she knew exactly how to get back up, and quickly. There wouldn't be a lot of time once that thing came after her. She landed on the ground and the rats scattered, squeaking and glaring with their beady little eyes. Above her, the volcano rumbled and ash rained down on her head. She threw her arms up to protect herself and hugged the side of her outcropping for protection. It burned through her long-sleeved shirt, or what was left of it. By now it was pretty tattered and torn. When the ash finally subsided, she ventured out, keeping a wary eye on the volcano.

"Chicken! Hey! Chicken!" she yelled, edging closer. She waved her arms and jumped, but the Basan didn't stir. Apparently it was used to sleeping through loud noises like volcano rumblings. "Chicken!" she screamed, but still nothing.

She couldn't go kick it like she really wanted, or she would never make it back to the rocks in time. She looked around her for anything she could use besides rats and rocks.

Rocks.

"Sometimes, Seven, I wonder about your intelligence." She scooped to pick up several cat-sized rocks, muttering to herself. "Okay, new plan. Throw the rock. Wake up the chicken. Climb the rocks, push the boulder. Easy peasy." She hefted the rock to her shoulder and threw it.

It made it about half the distance to the chicken, although it did scare a rat that looked like it might want to eat her. Seven muttered again and picked up another piece of broken lava. They were lighter than regular rocks, but she was counting on their jagged edges to poke the chicken and wake it up. She hurled the rock as hard as she could and it flew through the air, smacking the chicken in the chest.

It grunted and squawked under its breath, but didn't get up.

"Holy snowballs," Seven groaned. As if in agreement, the volcano above her spewed again—more than ash, this time. Drops of flaming lava rained around them and Seven yelped and dove for cover. She was out of time.

She raced closer to the chicken, grabbed her stone, and threw it hard, right at the chicken's face. It smashed into the forehead, bounced off the beak, and clattered to the ground. The red demon eyes snapped open and fixed on Seven.

"Oh dear."

She turned and ran, stumbling, as more lava rained on them. The chicken was on its feet, pounding after her, too fast because she had gotten too close. She was never going to make it back up. She had to think—think of a new plan—there had to be something . . .

She heard the boulder move, scraping across the rocks and rolling forward. She screeched and dove out of the way as it came crashing down—and landed right on the head of the chicken. The chicken fell with a mighty thud, shaking the ground and knocking Seven to her knees. The rats squealed in fear and scampered for cover.

The Basan's blue flames seemed to burn it away from the inside out until it was a giant chicken bonfire.

Seven looked up. Haran stood, bent over with his hands on his knees, breathing hard. He'd pushed the boulder. He'd followed her here and saved her life. Haran raised his head, met her astonished gaze, and he grinned, pale, shaking, and proud of himself.

"You're in so much trouble," she yelled. His grin broadened as he struggled to straighten. The chicken gave one last, horrendous squawk, and exploded in a mass of feathers and blue ash. At that exact moment, Seven felt the lock on her banshee half break and the warmth came flooding back.

And the volcano exploded.

Lava poured from the rim, racing down the side like anger itself coming after them. "Haran!" Seven screamed and leaped into the air. She was so grateful for the weightlessness that she could have cried, had there been time. Instead she snatched Haran off the ground and flew for the tunnel. The lava moved as quickly as she did, raining down from the sky and burning her back and hair. By the time she got to the Zimbabwe doorway and set Haran down by their packs, it had flowed over the entrance. She snatched him back up, grabbed their packs with the precious Fountain water, and went for the doorway on higher ground, hoping it would lead to Atlantis. It was in the back of a cave, and lava already pooled on the floor, but the doorway was in the wall. Hoping against hope that it would open, she flew straight at it. It shimmered to life and sucked them through right as they would have crashed into the black rock.

Inside, it was cool and dark. Seven set Haran on the ground and sank to the floor. "You're on fire," Haran said quietly. He patted Seven weakly with the sleeve of his shirt, putting out the flames she hadn't even noticed.

"I don't think I'd like to visit the Fountain of Youth again." Seven groaned and slid sideways.

"I'm okay with that. Do we have anything left to eat?"

Seven grinned, digging through their packs without sitting up. She handed him the last of their sandwiches and granola bars and double-checked the water bottle to make sure it was still tightly shut. "We'll have to . . . borrow . . . some food when we get to wherever this tunnel goes."

He split the sandwich and granola bar in half and handed it to her. They ate in exhausted silence before Haran slumped over, pushing his pack under his head for a pillow. "This is a good place to sleep, right?" he asked around a yawn.

Seven glanced around them. They were on a platform with ladders leading down to the tunnel. It disappeared below her and she had no idea what awaited them. But for the moment, they were safe. "Yeah, I think it is." She lay down next to him, putting a hand against him so she could feel him breathe. She was afraid to close her eyes, afraid to fall asleep because he might not be there when she woke up. She'd almost lost him today. She'd almost lost him and without Haran, she lost herself. She lost all the good in the world. She couldn't let that happen. "Sleep sweet, baby brother."

Seven didn't sleep. Her body ached and she'd passed exhausted and moved on to . . . what came after exhausted? Whatever it was, she'd passed it long ago, but sleep didn't come. Instead, she thought of Lady Kraken. She wished she could do research on her, the way her dad had taught her. She wished she could find her weaknesses so she'd know which of her powers to use against her, the way her mom had taught her.

It hit Seven, sometime late, late in the night, what this journey had been trying to teach her all along. She wasn't a banshee and she wasn't a human. She couldn't live her life shunning half of who she was. To find peace, to find happiness, to succeed and triumph over the things she faced, she had to embrace both sides of her.

That was how she would defeat Lady Kraken.

"Seven? I'm hungry. Should we go see what kind of food waits at the other end of this tunnel?" Haran's sleepy voice jarred her out of her thoughts, and she giggled. Even fighting for his life, her brother could only think about food.

They packed up their belongings in silence. Haran had deep circles under his eyes, but he didn't shake or tremble when he tried to move. Mostly he just looked really tired. Seven carried him over the edge instead of using the ladder, and they landed below. The ground was soft grass, and pink cherry trees lined the tunnel for as far as Seven could see. But there were no slippery slides. "Looks like we're walking," Haran said.

Seven shook her head. "No. We're not." She scooped him up under the arms and they flew through the tunnel. It wasn't empty—they passed other magical creatures. The first three groups Seven ignored, especially when they saw her coming and scattered, screaming. The fourth group of tiny little elf-things that Haran told her were called brownies, Seven finally stopped for. "You realize you're in a tunnel that only goes to an island with a volcano that just erupted, right?"

she asked quickly, before they could realize what she was and start screaming. "Also, there may or may not be more of Phoibos's minions waiting. I already had to defeat a giant chicken."

"Basan," Haran said, rolling his eyes.

"Banshee!" the brownies screamed, racing in circles in such a panic, some of them crashed into each and fell to the floor like fat little dolls. Their pointy hats toppled from their heads and their squealing shook the walls.

Seven sighed and crossed her arms, waiting for them to finish. It took a while.

"Knock it off already!" Haran yelled. "She's trying to help you. Does it look like she's scary at all?"

The brownies stopped and stared at him as if his words were entirely irrelevant. "Banshees are always beautiful," one whispered.

"That's what makes them so deadly."

Seven wasn't sure whether to be insulted or flattered. "How on earth do you think beauty makes a banshee deadly? We don't lure men to their deaths with our voice. We don't tempt them away from home with our looks. We cry when people die and make sure they make it to Death safely, without getting lost. Because you want to know what's terrifying?" She leaned down so she was almost eye level with the little men. "Lost souls. The things that cause mischief and possess people and scream and cry in the night? *Those* are scary. And banshees make sure there are as few of them as possible."

The brownies all shared wide-eyed, confused glances. Seven sat back and waited, because it seemed necessary for each brownie to exchange a look with every other brownie there. When they were done, one took two steps forward, avoiding eye-contact with Seven and focusing on Haran. "But we heard what the banshee did in Atlantis."

"Yeah? Well guess what the banshee did in Ireland? She fought off a pack of demons. And in Egypt. And in Africa. And in Japan she fought off a giant chicken and negotiated with Death himself."

"Basan," Seven said with a grin.

Haran sent her an exasperated scowl. "She's on her way to help save Atlantis. Not because she has to, but because it's the right thing to do. So stop treating her like she's going to eat you all alive!"

"Actually, I'm on my way because I have to. Otherwise I'd go home," Seven said conversationally, which earned her another scowl from Haran.

"We are sorry. We've never met a hybrid banshee before. Only heard rumors." They did look genuinely sorry, so Seven forgave them.

"Where does this tunnel go?" she asked, praying it was Atlantis. Hoping against hope that this was the last leg of their journey and that Haran would be well soon.

"Rio," the brownies answered in unison.

Seven dropped her head into her hands. "Crap."

"At least they have good food in Rio!" Haran said optimistically, sounding almost like his old self again.

Seven raised her head. "We don't have any money to buy that good food though. We're going to have to steal it. And you know how dad feels about stealing."

"Money?" several brownies said at once.

"You mean these?" They held out grubby little hands, in which were clutched bills and coins.

Seven leaned closer, bracing herself for their terror and flinching, but they seemed to be over the fright. Haran's lecture had worked, apparently. "These are pesos. Where did you get them?"

The brownie shrugged, brown eyes glittering mischievously. "We'll share." He thrust the rest of the pesos into Seven's hands. "And now we'll go."

"You really want to go that way?" Seven asked, raising an eyebrow. "It's very dangerous."

They all shared looks again, and then one motioned with his chubby hands and they gathered into a huddle and talked in fast little whispers. Seven stood, looking at Haran. He shrugged and continued to watch in amusement. Finally, a consensus seemed to be reached and they faced her. "We will go back to Rio. It is not far and there are other tunnels there."

Seven nodded. "All right then."

"We'll walk with you for a while," Haran said, raising his chin as if in defiance of his own weakness.

"I can carry you, Haran," Seven whispered, falling back to walk beside him as the little brownies led the way. They had to take about fifteen steps to her one, so it was slow going. Which seemed to work out better for her tired brother.

"I'm okay to walk for a while." He gave her a small smile and they walked in silence, listening to the brownies chatter.

Seven finally interrupted them. "Why are you trying to go to an unpopulated Japanese island?" she called. The brownies buzzed and bounced, swarming around her.

"Atlantis isn't safe."

"The hybrids are being thrown out."

"We don't fit in the human world."

"Ah." Seven nodded. "You were going there because there are no people. I see. You know . . . Santa's elves can always use some help in the North Pole."

The brownies buzzed more, their brown eyes alight with excitement as they muttered to each other.

"I can build toys."

"I like reindeer."

"White is a good color on me."

"It's a good plan," Haran said. Seven nodded, glancing over at him. He was pale and starting to shake.

"It's time for us to go, little guys. Can you tell me how to find the gate to Atlantis when I get to Rio?" Seven knelt in front of them, meeting each gaze, which seemed really important to them. She didn't know why, but she wanted them to know she was grateful for their help.

"It's in the Tijuca Forest."

"You'll find it in the mountainous region."

"Walk through the waterfall."

Seven nodded. She'd heard of the Tijuca Forest. Arguably the largest urban forest in the world—which meant it was right in the middle of the city. Originally, the rainforest in Rio had been torn down to build coffee farms, but several decades ago, the citizens had re-planted millions and millions of trees to re-grow the rainforest. "Okay. Thank you. Thank you so much."

She turned to Haran. "Are you ready for

some Brazilian food, little brother?"

He rubbed his stomach with a pained look. "At this point I'd eat dog food, Sev. Let's get moving."

CHAPTER THIRTEEN: ROLLING RIO RAINS

They emerged from the tunnel in the middle of a river. Instead of stepping through or climbing up like they had to in all the others, this entrance grabbed them and threw them—straight through the water and onto the white sand of the beach. "Holy crap!" Seven gasped. She looked around quickly to see who noticed them, but of the gazillion people in Rio, none of them had been watching when the banshee and her human brother were spit out of the ocean. "Are you okay?" she asked Haran, wringing the salty water from her bright red curls. He nodded, still lying on the sand, staring at the sky. It was night here, and the stars were somewhere above, but the lights from the city were so bright Seven could barely see them. She sat back on her knees and looked around, waiting for Phoibos's minions to come popping out of the sand after them. None did.

Yet.

She could see the giant outcropping of rock that Rio was so famous for. They sat on the curve of beach she'd seen in pictures, with the city behind them. Somewhere beyond the bustle of the city was the Tijuca Forest. "Okay. We just gotta make it through the city to the forest, and then somehow figure out where the gate to Atlantis is in the twelve square miles of trees and mountains. No problem."

"Food first." Haran sat up and looked eagerly toward the city.

"Yes. Food first." She pulled her pack off her back and dumped everything out, wrung out as much water as she could, and then loaded it all back in. She still had her phone—it still had a very dead battery, and she was pretty sure she wouldn't get service on the other side of the world. But she tucked it back in her pack anyway, in case she ever made it home. For the eight hundredth time, she checked Haran's water bottle to make sure it wasn't leaking.

Then she did the whole thing over again with Haran's pack. By the time she was finished, she could hear Haran's stomach growling, so she pulled him to his feet and slung both their packs over her shoulder. "Come on, let's see if we can brave the streets of Rio for some food."

Rio was not a place for children wandering around on their own. It was big and loud and there were a ton of people. She could see the mountain and the giant statue of Jesus in the distance. If she remembered right, and she was pretty sure she did because her dad had quizzed her on it a gazillion times, that super famous statue stood in the Tijuca Forest. So she made her way toward that while looking for a street vendor or market or anything selling food.

Haran, of course, found it first. It was a little market selling something that smelled really, really good. Seven didn't speak Portuguese, so she pointed to the soup and held out her money. She realized that this man could very well swindle her out of everything she had, but he took pity on her instead. He counted her money and set aside what she was assuming was the price for the soup. She held up two fingers, hoping he'd realize she wanted two bowls. He smiled and nodded, taking more money and handing her the rest. While he was dishing up their soup, she saw the breads and pastries sitting on the counter. "Those look good," she said to Haran.

"Oh, you speak English?" the man asked. Between his very strong Portuguese accent and her Irish accent, it was a wonder they could understand each other at all. But understand they did.

"Yes sir," she answered, blushing at the way her words rolled differently from her tongue. "We're travelling from Ireland."

He studied her as he handed her the bowl. "Where are your parents?"

Seven realized this was the first time she'd spoken to a human since she'd left her dad, and she wasn't prepared for how to answer him. Haran, apparently, was. "Our moms are both gone. We can't find them."

Nice, kid. Way to tell the truth in a totally

misleading way!

"Do you need me to alert the authorities?" the man asked, his thick black eyebrows rose in alarm.

"No, no." Seven shook her head violently. "No, we know where we're going. We're just very hungry and we have a long walk ahead of us."

The man's eyes hardened. "Someone should ring their necks."

Haran smiled faintly, the circles under his eyes more pronounced. "I'm sure it isn't their choice."

At the man's confused look, Seven hurriedly changed the subject. "Do I have enough money to buy some of those?" She pointed at the breads and treats she'd been eying earlier.

"Those and your feijoada, yes." He started packing up the bread, nodding.

"The feijo . . . huh?"

He chuckled. "Feijoada. Your soup. It's a national food of Rio. You will love it." He handed Seven her bag, and she tucked it into her backpack for later. Then she took the soup and plastic spoons and handed him her money. He counted out the correct amount and handed her the change.

"Thank you so much," Seven murmured. Tears of gratitude for his kindness burned her eyes as she backed away, the soup clutched to her chest so she wouldn't spill it.

"Are you sure you're okay?" he asked gently.

Seven nodded and fled the market, Haran on her heels. "Wow. Rio people are nice," he said as they wandered into a huge city park. Seven sat on the grass, prying the lid from her food. It smelled delicious, especially since they hadn't eaten since the night before, and they'd had nothing warm to eat in days. Haran leaned against her, already shaking from exertion.

"They are nice," Seven said. "This is yummy. It's better than yummy—it's delicious." She was trying to sound positive and bright and strong. She was trying not to let him know how scared she was.

Haran slurped his soup. "Yeah it is." He took another bite and tipped his head so he could see her face. "Seven?"

"Hmm?"

"What do you think Dad is doing right now?"

Seven's heart clenched tightly. She knew what he was doing. He was pacing the living room, wondering why she hadn't called, wondering if they were even alive. He was worried sick. And she wanted to go home. So, so much. She was so homesick it felt like a real live thing, eating away at her heart. But that wasn't what Haran needed to hear. "I think he's probably watching that crime show on TV that he won't watch while we're awake because he thinks it will rot our minds or scare us or whatever he's always saying. And he's probably wandering around in his bathrobe because we're not there to make him get dressed. His hair is probably a mess and he's forgotten to brush his teeth. Parents need children to keep them in line."

Haran snickered. "I thought it was the other way around."

Seven looked down at him and smiled. "That's what they want you to think."

"I wonder if anyone at school has beaten my score in the mythology game," Haran said. "I worked really hard to get the highest score."

"No way. And now, when we go back, you'll have hands-on experience with different myths from all over the world. No one is gonna hold a candle to you."

She felt his jaw move against her shoulder as he grinned. They ate quietly, watching the people racing by in their busy lives. It was so different than their small village in Ireland. Or the sandy desert of Egypt. Or the savannah of Africa. And the Japanese island was like a world of its own. All these places were completely unique from one another. "If we hadn't had to come on this journey, we'd never have seen any of these wonders. I'd never know how amazing life outside of Ireland could be."

"See? It's a good thing I almost died."

Seven snorted. "Not even close. But maybe it's a good thing we came to help Atlantis."

They finished their soup just as it started to rain. If raining was like opening the sky and pouring sheets of water on their heads. For some reason, she'd assumed it didn't rain in Rio. Apparently, they had a rainy season and she and

Haran were lucky enough to be caught in it. Seven held her bag over Haran's head. "Well this is miserable."

"Yeah. Maybe we should find somewhere to sleep?" Haran asked, "Away from all the people," he looked around nervously—"and potential bad guys?"

"Maybe with the cover of darkness and this thick rain I can risk flying us to the forest and we can find the gate. They seem safe places to sleep." Haran nodded and stood up, gathering his bowl and spoon. Seven took them and ran over to the trash can, watching for people along the way. No one seemed to want to be out in the rain, and if anyone was watching from the windows, well…

They were too far away to do anything if they happened to see a girl flying her brother through the downpour.

She looped her arms through his and leaped into the sky, relishing the return of her banshee half. It was difficult in the rain. The fat drops clung to her lashes and blurred her vision and the rain threw off her balance. But they managed to make it out of the city, past the giant statue of

Jesus—

And into the forest.

With the thick trees above them, Seven finally dropped to the ground. "I think there are a lot of wild animals here, so stay close."

Haran sighed. "It's a rainforest, Sev. Of course there are a lot of wild animals here."

She pulled a face at him and he grinned as they started walking. "At least the thick trees keep most of the rain off us," she said optimistically. Flying would be impossible here because the trees were so close together. She wished she could leave Haran somewhere safe so she could wander around lost trying to find a small waterfall, but there were too many dangers. Leaving him wasn't an option.

So they walked slowly. Very slowly. The heavy rains sounded like hail on the giant leaves above them, and the ground under their feet became slick. In many places, she could see the mountain starting to slide. She swallowed. The sooner they found the gate, the better.

"The brownies said it was behind a waterfall. So if we find a river, we'll follow it. No problem,"

Haran said, scanning the darkness like the river might pop up out of the ground in front of them.

"Yeah. We'll find the river. No problem." Seven didn't want to mention that there were a ton of rivers in Brazil. Instead, she looped his arm around her shoulder and held as much of his weight as she could while they wandered.

For hours.

And hours.

As her feet began to throb and her back had long ago started to ache, she realized something was following them.

Evil dog beasts, shadowy demons, dog-lizard things, and giant chickens were all very scary. But she'd faced all of them in the daylight. At night, terror had a whole new meaning. She couldn't see anything, but she felt it. Felt eyes on her back, but when she looked over her shoulder, there was nothing there. And she certainly couldn't hear anything over the sound of the rain. There was nothing she could do but keep moving. "Maybe we can see more from the top of that hill over there." Haran pointed. His entire arm shook with complete exhaustion, although he hadn't complained once. Seven looked to see, and her heart sank. The hill would be impossible to climb, but the trees were too close together for her to carry him while she flew. They wouldn't fit.

Haran glanced at her and then dropped his arm and headed toward the hill, climbing on his hands and feet up the side. She quickly followed him. The ground was slick and fell away under her hands. There was nothing stable to hold on to. Haran had made it about five feet up when the ground caved and he toppled backward on top of her. She caught him, flying into the air to avoid crashing backward. "Are you okay?" she asked as she slammed into a tree.

"Yeah," he panted. "Are you?"

Seven nodded and set him down as high as she could reach, and they started climbing. She hadn't gone far when she felt the ground sliding again. She just had time to think she needed to warn Haran when the entire hillside collapsed, crashing in one giant mudslide backward. Trees and rocks were carried with it, rolling over her and Haran both. She screamed, which was a bad idea, because that shook everything else loose, and they rode the mudslide, half-buried, for several hundred feet. "Haran!" she cried, reaching for his hand. His entire body was under mud, with only his fingers visible. She struggled to stay on top of the slide as she grasped his fingers and pulled.

A falling tree landed hard against her back and slid over the top of her, shoving her deeper into the mud. She kept a tight grip on Haran's fingers and fought her way to the surface again.

Frantic, she dug down deep into her banshee half and grabbed the warmth for her eyes. The flames burst free and lit up the night, slicing through the mud and the trees around Haran. It bubbled and sizzled as she pulled her brother up, up, up out of the muck holding him hostage, to the surface where he choked and gagged and spit mud from his mouth.

The slide finally stopped, and Haran crawled into her lap and for the first time in their entire journey, he cried. He curled against her and sobbed until her heart broke and everything in her shattered, and she just wanted to take him home.

But if she took him home, he would die.

So instead she held him tight in her mud-covered arms, rocked him back and forth, and she sang the ancient Celtic verse her mother had taught her. Her ghost army came, but there was nothing to fight so instead they surrounded her and Haran in a tight circle and stood watch through the night. Haran, finally sobbed himself to sleep, and Seven slumped over him, letting sleep take her as well.

CHAPTER FOURTEEN:
A BIGFOOT BY
ANY OTHER NAME

Seven, something approaches. Should we attack?"

These were not the words Seven had hoped to awaken to. She scrubbed her eyes, forcing her spine to straighten after being slumped over all night. Not the best way to get adequate rest, really. She brushed her soggy curls out of her face and peered around her through the dimness. The sun was rising; she could tell because of the weak light attempting to find its way through the leaves, but it was still very dark in the forest. It was hard to distinguish anything in the shadows. "I don't see—I—where—?" Her words were slurred in her sleepy panic.

Grandmother Macfarland pointed silently through the forest. Seven squinted into the darkness, looking for the now-familiar glowing red eyes of Phoibos's minions. "I don't see anything," she whispered.

"It comes closer."

Seven sighed, sliding out from under a still-sleeping Haran. What would Phoibos send this time? It would be really hard to top a giant, flame-shooting chicken. At least this time, she had her banshee powers. And her human strength. Using them together, she could beat anything if she had to.

She just really wished she didn't have to.

She scanned the surrounding trees, safely within the protection of her ghosts. "I still don't see anything," she murmured. No red, glowing eyes. Nothing. But then the smell hit her. "Oh dear," she gasped, covering her nose with her hand. "What is that?" It smelled like something dead and rotting—although not quite as bad as the Abuki in Africa. She ventured away from Haran, glancing at her ghosts. "Protect him, please? I'm going to see what I can find."

"Be careful, little banshee," Grandfather Bailey said as the rest of them tightened their circle around Haran. She nodded and set off into the darkness. The rain had stopped, thankfully, and the ground was spongy in the humidity. It sucked at her tennis shoes with every step, making weird slurping noises when she pulled her feet free. The overlapping giant leaves created an umbrella ceiling, which completely blocked out the rising sun. The only thing she could see in the shadows was the reflection of many eyes peering at her through the undergrowth. These eyes weren't demonic, though—just animals. Lots of animals. She remembered reading that there were a ton of endangered species here that could only be found in the Tijuca Forest. So . . . she probably needed to be careful not to kill any of them. She definitely didn't want to be a poacher or something. Although if a jaguar tried to eat her, she'd have to defend herself. Because getting eaten by a jaguar wasn't on her agenda for the day.

She was so busy watching for man-eating creatures that she didn't realize the smell had gotten overwhelmingly strong until she smashed right into something big and solid and furry.

And very, very stinky.

She squealed and danced backward. She tripped over a root and fell, catching herself at the last second. She flew to her feet, finally getting a good look at the thing she'd crashed into.

Big Foot.

She'd crashed into Big Foot.

She screeched, knocking it backward, and it bellowed, throwing its hands up to protect its face. "Banshee!" it screamed in its guttural voice.

"Wait! Wait—you're—you're afraid of me?" she tipped her head sideways, watching it suspiciously. This wasn't what she'd been expecting at all.

"Banshee bad. Banshees hurt." The Big Foot thing peeked through its fingers at her.

She ignored that. Narrowing her eyes, she said, "You weren't sent by Phoibos to capture me?"

"Who Phoibos?" It slowly lowered its hairy hands. It didn't have the glowing red eyes of

Phoibos's other minions. It had milky brown eyes and a very monkey-like face. She might have even mistaken it for a gorilla, except that it was huge and didn't have the super long arms that a gorilla did. It had more of a human-like body, except with matted, dirty and smelly hair.

"Never mind. You aren't here to hurt me?"

"You banshee. Banshee bad. Banshee hurts."

She shook her head. "No, banshees aren't bad. They don't hurt unless you hurt them first. Are you Big Foot?"

"Me Mapinguari. Big Foot cousin."

"I—I see. Are you going to eat me?" Seven planted her hands on her hips and tried to look brave. She was fairly positive she failed, given that she was staring down a ten foot tall ape-like creature, but it was worth a shot.

"Mapinguari don't eat people." He looked offended at the thought, his small chin pulled in tight and his hairy brows lowered.

"Then why have you been following us?" Seven asked. She glanced over her shoulder, but she couldn't see Haran through the thick trees. She just had to have faith in her ghosts. She'd feel a lot better if she could get back to him, though.

"Mapinguari curious. Bad lady told Mapinguari to stop banshee. But Mapinguari scared of banshee."

Lady Kraken. She must have sent this creature to stop her. She hadn't counted on Seven's reputation preceding her. For once, it wasn't so bad being known as a terrifying monster. Or was it possible Lady Kraken was the only magical creature ever to *not* realize how scary banshees were? It was sure seeming like it.

"You don't have to be afraid of me if you aren't going to hurt me. My brother and I, we're trying to get to Atlantis. To help stop the bad man. But my brother is very sick and we can't find the gate. Can you help us? If I promise not to hurt you?"

"Banshee . . . be Mapinguari friend?"

In those few vulnerable words, Seven understood it all. He was like her—a mystery, because he was rare. And he had a reputation for being big and terrifying, and his smell . . . well, no one would come near him. Just like her, minus the smell.

She hoped.

She had no pets, she had no friends. Magical creatures were terrified of her, and humans avoided her. How many times had her heart been broken because of their fear? "Yes, banshee will be Mapinguari's friend."

He leaped once and clapped his hands, the sound shaking the trees around them. Little animals scurried out from their hiding places, darting in fear through the darkness. "Mapinguari never had friend before."

She smiled. "Then I'm happy to be the first. I need to check on my brother. Would you like to come?"

The smile dissolved from the creature's ape-like face. "Brother hurt Mapinguari?"

Seven chuckled. "No. Not even close. My brother is the kindest person I've ever met." She turned and walked back toward their mudslide, motioning him to follow. "He's very sick. I have to get him to Atlantis to save him."

"Atlantis gates closed."

How did he even know this? She was fairly positive her new Mapinguari friend did not have a tablet or access to SplashSpace. "I know. I have to open it."

"It guarded. By angry Kraken lady."

Seven smirked, before rearranging her face to look up at him. "Yes, I know. I'm supposed to defeat her."

"She's angry."

"Yes, I've heard." They found their way back to the mudslide, and Seven slid awkwardly down to her ghosts, most of whom raised their weapons, glaring dangerously.

The Mapinguari shrieked in fear and stumbled backward, banging into trees before he turned to run.

"Wait!" She held her hands out, but she wasn't sure to whom. First, the ghosts. "He's a friend!"

Then she hurried after her ape-creature. "Wait! They're just protecting my brother! They won't hurt you!" He was huddled behind a wide tree trunk, mostly obscured by the bush. No wonder no one could ever get a good look at these creatures. They blended perfectly with their surroundings. She would have run right past if not for his sobs. She skidded to a stop and turned, squatting on her haunches next to him. "Hey. I'm sorry. They didn't mean to scare you."

"Banshee not friend."

"Banshee *is* friend." She reached out and stroked his hairy hand, curling her fist around one of his fingers. "Every time we turn around, someone is attacking us. They didn't know you aren't a bad guy. Come back with me and I'll introduce you."

He shook his head so violently, twigs and dirt flew out of his fur, spattering her face. She would care, if she wasn't positive she was already covered in much worse. "Please?" She pulled out her best puppy dog look, the one she gave her dad when he was determined not to buy her a new book and she was desperate to have one.

The Mapinguari peeked through his fingers at her. She smiled encouragingly. "Ghosts won't hurt Mapinguari?"

She shook her head, feeling twigs and dirt fly free. She couldn't wait to go home and have a nice long shower. After she hugged her dad.

For an eternity.

She would give anything to be able to talk to her dad right this second. But her phone wouldn't work here, and unless he'd mastered conversations by brainwaves while she'd been gone, a conversation just wasn't possible.

"Do you have a name?" she asked around the sudden lump in her throat. The Mapinguari looked at her blankly so she continued, "A home? A family?"

He shook his head, fat tears falling down his furry face. "Okay then. Let's give you a name. How about . . . Mappy?"

He smiled, a big grin splitting his face as he dropped his hands and nodded eagerly.

"Good. Mappy it is. Where is your family?"

"Mappy doesn't have family. Mappy alone."

Seven thought about the forests surrounding her village. She thought about Akie, already there. What was one more mythical creature? "When I go back to Ireland, will you come home with us?" *I'm sure Dad is fine with it.* "There are deep forests with lots of trees and places to hide. You won't be alone anymore."

The smile transformed him. He wasn't big

and scary any more. He was kind and sweet. She didn't think about the consequences of taking a mythical creature out of his habitat and placing him somewhere else. She was sure there would be some. Maybe she'd get some sort of magical fine or punishment. But she didn't care. That smile made it worth it. "Now I really need to get back to my brother." She looked hopefully at him. "Will you come?"

He nodded and rose, towering over her, his head in the lower branches of the trees. She turned and hurried back to Haran, the ghosts watching warily but not raising their weapons. She could see weariness in their translucent faces. It made them tired to be here with her. How could she not have realized that? "You can go home now. I think we're okay," she told them.

Even then, when she'd given them permission, they hesitated. Protecting her. "You are very loyal friends. I love you all." She wiped tears from her cheeks, but good tears—like when she gave her dad his Father's Day card and he'd cried. They were those kinds of tears.

"Mappy take care of banshee now," he said,

approaching shyly. He slipped a little on the mud, and looked up with panicked eyes, expecting to be met with the sharp ends of their swords. But if Seven trusted him, so did they. They waved once and were gone, back home to rest after watching over Seven and Haran all night long.

She glanced at her little brother. He still slept. Through it all, he hadn't stirred. That was not a good sign. He'd always been an amazingly light sleeper. They had to have a fan in his room all the time to drown out random normal-house noises and neighbor dogs barking, or he couldn't sleep at all. Kneeling next to him, she checked with shaking hands to make sure he was still breathing, then she leaned close to listen to his heart. "He's getting weaker. I think our fight with the mudslide yesterday cost him too much. We need to get to Atlantis."

"Mappy take you. Mappy know way."

Seven nodded, almost sobbing with relief at his words. He knew the way. No more wandering lost. She bent to pick up Haran, her back already protesting after their fall down the mountain the day before and sleeping all slumped over. She didn't want to wake him—not when he so desperately needed sleep. "Haran," she whispered.

She held her breath until he opened his eyes. The shadows were deeper and darker in his pale face, so that they almost looked like bruises now. He gave her a weak smile. "Is it morning already—" And then he screamed, because his eyes had moved past Seven to Mappy. He tried to point or call out a warning but his arm was too weak, so it flopped limply at his side.

Seven expected Mappy to run again, and this time she didn't have her ghosts to protect Haran while she ran after him. But Mappy didn't move. Instead he raised one big hand slowly in greeting. "Hi."

"Big Foot?" Haran gasped.

Seven looked over her shoulder at Mappy with a smile before turning back to Haran. "Big Foot's cousin. He's here to help us. And . . . then we're taking him home with us."

Haran's eyes lit, just a little, so that he reminded her of the old Haran, before Death had gotten hold of him. "Cool."

She giggled. "Yeah. Do you think Dad will like that?"

Haran tipped his head to the side so he could see Mappy around Seven. "Hi. Dad will love you."

"I know, right?" Seven giggled, so happy that Haran was talking that her laughter sounded a little crazy. "Are you hungry? We should probably eat something before we go." Above them, thunder rolled, and she could hear the rain smashing against the umbrella leaves. Rain meant mudslides. She didn't want to risk that again.

Haran, evidently, was in agreement, because he struggled to his feet and stood swaying in the darkness. "Maybe we could eat later."

CHAPTER FIFTEEN:
MAPPY THE FOREST GUIDE

Mappy help?" Mappy stepped forward, arms half-raised but with fear of rejection written all over his face.

Seven breathed a sigh of relief. She wouldn't have to carry Haran. "That would be fantastic, Mappy." Haran nodded silently and Mappy scooped him up like some kind of big baby, cradling him against his chest. Seven hurriedly dug out some pastries from the night before and handed one to her brother. "Mappy? Do you like treats?" she asked, holding one out for him, too.

Mappy shook his head as he set off with long strides across the forest floor, winding his way through trees like he wasn't as big as the side of a barn. "Mappy eat trees." He glanced over his shoulder to make sure Seven was following him. "Follow Mappy home? Then to gate."

She nodded, hoping it wasn't too far out of the way. She was already so tired, and Haran didn't have a lot of time. But it wasn't like she had a choice. He was the only one who knew where the gate was. They'd spent hours and hours searching the day before and hadn't found even a hint of a gate or tunnel anywhere. She ate her pastry silently and pretended not to notice how muddy the forest floor was getting as the rain ran down the mountainside in mini rivers. It would have been easy to lose Mappy in the semi-darkness. He blended so well with the forest that if Seven blinked for too long, he'd disappear completely. So she stayed close, sometimes holding on to his dirty fur when she got worried. They passed the eyes again, many eyes all staring at them through the underbrush. She heard low growls and rustling through the rain, but apparently these creatures were more scared of Mappy than they were of a little banshee. Nothing attacked, and the only thing she had to worry about for the next hour or so was the slippery ground under their feet.

But Mappy knew where to step, and she followed in his footsteps. "Mappy, you said the Lady Kraken is angry. Do you know anything else about her?" *See, Dad? I'm doing my research. You should be proud.*

Mappy paused, raising his nose to the air, reminding Seven of a dog testing an incoming scent. She inched closer, wondering what might be coming. But Mappy skipped off, so it must not have been anything serious. She hurried to catch up. "Kraken. Lots of legs. Big. Bigger than Mappy. Bigger than Mappy house." He nodded, as if agreeing with himself, and turned sharply to the left, narrowly avoiding running into trees set close together. Seven danced around them and hurried after him.

"Slow. Slow and angry. More angry, more slow." Mappy continued when she got closer.

"You mean, the madder she gets, the slower she gets?" Mappy nodded and Seven did a happy little dance. That could definitely come in handy. Then she had to focus on not falling, because the undergrowth was slipping and sliding under the onslaught of rain water. She didn't speak again for several minutes, not until Mappy ducked through a tunnel of trees and disappeared. She raced to catch up, hurrying through the tangled tunnel, and found herself in a giant cave, lit by glow worms along the ceiling. Sort of like track lighting, *au natural*. "Wow."

"This Mappy's home." Mappy laid Haran down on a bed of huge umbrella leaves. Haran smiled over at her but didn't say anything.

"It's lovely."

Mappy shrugged, something so human that it startled Seven for a minute. "It home. Humans can't find it. Rain can't find it." It was true. It was dry here, and warm. Haran shivered on his nest, pulling his legs up to his chest and resting his head on his knees.

She knelt next to him. "Eat, Haran. And maybe drink a little more of the water. This will all be over soon." Haran didn't raise his head, but turned so he could see her and nodded tiredly. She dropped their bags off her shoulder and dug through them, finding more pastries and the precious water. "Just a sip," she said, pouring a little into the cap. Haran nodded again and took it, swallowing the water. Immediately she could see improvement—not a lot, but enough that he would make it to the gate.

She hoped.

She watched him eat and forced a little down her own throat. Now that they were so close, she was nervous. No, nervous was an understatement. More like . . . maybe there were ten thousand lightning bugs all fighting for space in her stomach. If she failed . . . if she didn't defeat Lady Kraken . . .

Haran would die.

Atlantis would be closed off. Magic would die.

She swallowed hard. *No point thinking of the negative, Sev.* Her dad's voice was welcome in her head—how many times had he told her that when she faced a math test she was certain she'd fail, or a soul she didn't want to take? She straightened her spine and raised her chin. Yes, she was stubborn. She could do this.

Mappy gathered a few little trinkets—a doll,

ragged and worn and muddy that got lost in his big palm. An old broken tea cup. A mirror, long since cracked in many places. He put them in a leaf that he folded expertly like a knapsack on a stick. Seven raised an eyebrow. She'd seen such a thing in cartoons before, but never in real life. "Mappy ready."

Seven sucked in a deep breath. "Okay. Can you carry Haran again?" Mappy nodded, and she swapped him his knapsack for her brother. She felt a little like a packhorse with her backpack, Haran's backpack, and Mappy's knapsack slung over her shoulder. And everything was wet and soggy and humid. Her curls were a disastrous mixture of frizz and mud and tangles. She'd be very glad to get out of this place and on to somewhere less . . . wet.

Mappy swept out of the cave, Haran clutched to his chest. They ducked through the tangled tunnel of trees, Seven on his heels. "The little elf things told us—"

"Brownies," Haran said with an exaggerated sigh.

"Right, brownies. They told us the gate

entrance was through a waterfall. We tried to follow the river but we got caught in the mudslide."

"Brownies pesky," was all Mappy said. He had to take short steps with his long legs, because the trees were so thick and close together here. It took them quite a while to work their way through the dense undergrowth, and by the time they found the river, the sun was high in the sky, or at least Seven was pretty sure it was high in the sky—it was hard to tell because of the canopy above them and the clouds rolling in and out, drenching them every chance.

The little river ran next to them, small enough that Seven could easily jump from one side to the other. She could see animals approaching cautiously in the distance to drink, but they scattered as soon as Mappy got close. Who would have thought she'd find a kindred spirit in Big Foot's cousin?

"Don't play in water," Mappy said over his shoulder, stepping carefully over the stream. "Mean fishies bite." He held up one hand, where half of one of his huge fingers seemed to be missing.

"Piranhas?" Seven asked.

Mappy shrugged. "Mean. Not pretty."

Seven smiled. No, piranhas were definitely not pretty fishies with their under-bite and big, sharp teeth. And scales. Seven shivered. She wasn't a fan of fish. Especially fish that could eat her. Seven leaped, flying a little just to be safe, and cleared the stream. She peeked down at the stream as she went over—it was muddy and swarming with a bunch of small, brown bodies. She landed safely on the other side as a squeal rose from upstream. Jerking toward it, she watched in horror as a small pig-looking thing was caught and dragged in. Before she could see too much, she squinched her eyes tightly and hurried after Mappy.

"Mappy . . . " Haran started. He was staring at something over Seven's shoulder. The hair on the back of her neck stood up. They were being followed. "Are there jaguars in this forest?"

"Yep," Mappy said cheerfully. "Jaguars pretty. Sharp teeth."

"Will they bother you?" Haran asked

nervously. His eyes were like big saucers in his head. Above them, even the brightly-colored birds were silent, watching and waiting.

"Sometimes. Mappy too big, mostly."

But Seven wasn't. She felt the thing without even turning around, before Haran screamed, before she heard the low rumble of a growl in its chest. She whirled, the heat already exploding from her eyes, and hit the jaguar as it leaped for her. Claws outstretched, teeth bared. And now . . . slightly fried. It screamed in pain and tumbled out of the air, crashing into the mud that promptly put out the sparks in its burning fur. It looked at Seven like she was the meanest creature ever—as if it hadn't been about to tear her to shreds. "Well, now you know why the animals in Ireland avoid me," she told it. With an angry huff, she turned and hurried after Mappy.

"You're getting pretty quick with those magical powers of yours," Haran said, nodding his approval. Seven smiled. Something had happened on this journey. The two halves of her had clicked together to make one whole Seven.

They stomped through the forest for several

more minutes. Where trees were too tight for Mappy to fit through, he knocked them out of the way. It was much faster than when she and Haran had been wandering aimlessly the day before. Seven had been looking for a huge waterfall, falling at least a hundred feet. Everything in this forest seemed larger than life, so why wouldn't the gate to Atlantis be?

Instead, Mappy led them along a stream. There was no mighty roar to call them to the gate, as a big waterfall would have had. No, the gate seemed to be hidden behind a curtain of water that only fell about ten feet and was only about three feet wide. "This is it? This is the gate we've been looking for?" Seven asked, staring at the cascading water.

Mappy nodded cheerfully.

Well, the brownies certainly could have been more specific in their description. She nodded and started toward it. Time was wasting. She had a Kraken to defeat and a brother to save.

Mappy's big hand shot out and caught her as her foot was poised over the stream, just ready to step in. "Mean fishies." He nodded with his chin and Seven looked down. Sharp teeth snapped at her shoe and she shrieked, jerking away.

"What are they doing here?" she gasped. Good grief, she'd nearly lost the sole of her favorite shoe. Not to mention the only shoes she had with her on this insane little journey.

Mappy gave her a look that clearly said he thought she was crazy. "They live here."

"But the water—it's only, like, a foot deep!" She could see the bottom, teaming with mud and moss and rocks.

Mappy shrugged. "Mean fishies aren't picky."

Well, that much was true. They'd almost eaten her shoe. Haran peered around Mappy's shoulder to see Seven and the stream. "So . . . how do we get through if the piranhas eat us as soon as we touch the water?"

"Maybe we run really fast?" Mappy asked, scratching his furry head.

Seven studied the fish, which leaped and snapped out of the water, as if angry that she'd stolen their meal. How rude of her to think she needed her foot more than they did. The entire stream was full of sharp teeth and scales. She tried to remember if piranhas were family fish or if they traveled in packs or if the stream was just always packed full of lethal fish. There was no way they could make it through the gate before the fish attacked—even if she flew. The fish could jump too high. How amusing that the one thing stopping them from getting to Atlantis wasn't even magical. And by amusing, she meant completely not amusing at all. No, somehow, they needed the fish *out* of the water so they could get in it. But how could they possibly do that?

The idea came out of her mouth before she had even realized it was an actual thought. "I blow them out of the water."

CHAPTER SIXTEEN:
TEETH VERSUS SCREAM

"O kay. Here's what I'm going to do." She backed up, pulling Mappy and Haran with her while she glared at the toothy fish. Yeah. She could totally do this without any of them dying. No problem. "Mappy, I'm going to scream. We'll have to find something to plug your ears . . ." she glanced around, ignoring Mappy's look of sheer terror.

"Why banshee want to scream at Mappy?" he asked, alarmed.

She shook her head as she stooped to scoop some mud onto her fingers. "No, I'm not going to scream at you. I'm going to scream at the fish. And blow them out of the water. And hold the rest of them off until we can get in to the gate."

She squinted up at him. "Easy Peasy, right?"

Haran snorted.

She frowned at him before rising, the mud gooped on her finger. "I'm going to put this in your ears, Mappy. We'll wash it out as soon as we get to safety." She searched his face. "Okay?"

"Banshee won't hurt Mappy?"

She shook her head again and reached up, but even on her tiptoes she couldn't reach his ears. Dang tiny banshee legs. She lifted herself into the air, loving the weightlessness flying gave her even as she banged her head on low hanging branches. Water slid from the leaves and ran down the back of her hoodie. She gasped, catching and holding the shriek that threatened to escape. That would be all Mappy needed—to get shrieked at. He was already scared of her as it was. As she worked, she explained the plan. "Mappy, as soon as I start screaming, I need you to run for the gate. Because I can blow these toothy fishies out of the water, but more will come as soon as I stop screaming. So we have to move fast. Okay?" She waited until he met her eyes and nodded so that she knew he understood.

She'd hate for him to get bitten. Or eaten. She just hoped on the other side of that waterfall was dry land that toothy fishies couldn't get up on.

Carefully, she coated his ears with mud and stuck some leaves over them for good measure. She sat back and surveyed her handiwork. "Nice. That'll do," she said with a smile. Then she turned to Haran.

"Not a chance. I'll cover my own ears, thanks." He scowled at her, holding his hands out like that would stop her if she really wanted to stick mud in his ears.

"Haran, do it. It's funny," Mappy said loudly with what sounded like a giggle as he poked at his own ears. Mapinguaries giggled. Who would have thought?

Haran shook his head and Seven sighed. Would it really be so bad to have mud in his ears? "Fine. Get ready."

She turned and faced the little stream full of deadly fish. Glancing over her shoulder, she said, "All set?"

Mappy stared blankly at her. Haran tapped him on the shoulder and waited until Mappy looked at him to yell, "She's gonna scream now. Get ready to run!" Mappy's eyes widened and he nodded enthusiastically, tightening his grip on Haran. Her brother covered his ears and met her gaze, also nodding to signal she could go ahead.

She sucked in a deep breath and closed her eyes, making sure she had a tight grip on her banshee half before she opened her mouth. She screamed, finally opening her eyes to watch the water explode from the little stream. The piranhas flew out, littering the trees and the mud and the bushes, flopping and snapping angrily.

"Go, go, go!" Haran screeched, and Seven heard Mappy crashing through the underbrush and into the now-empty stream bed. The waterfall crashed over him and he let out a surprised yell. Hopefully because it was cold and not because he was being eaten alive. Seven kept screaming, the sound tearing at her throat like a bunch of small knives chopping up her insides. She backed up quickly, holding the water at bay as she leaped into the stream bed and followed Mappy through the waterfall. It was indeed frigid, and if she hadn't already been screaming, she definitely would have as it poured over her head. As soon as she made it through, she stopped screaming. It was a huge relief to her aching throat.

She sloshed through the stream toward the bank, but she was too slow. She felt the sharp teeth snap at her high tops and she squealed, leaping out of the water with the evil little fish still attached to her favorite shoe. She kicked and the fish jerked free, flying across the little cave to smack into the wall. It fell to the ground and flopped toward Mappy, teeth snapping. Mappy bellowed and dove for the far side of the cave.

And disappeared.

"Well, I suppose that's the gate then," Seven muttered as she landed on the sandy floor and bent to survey the damage on her shoe. Her dad was definitely going to have to buy her a new pair. This made her sad and excited at the same time. The joys of being a teenage girl. She glared one last time at the evil fish for good measure before ducking through the gate.

She stood on a dirt landing. She'd been hoping for the slippery slides, but apparently they were only for select surface tunnels. This one had a long, very ancient looking ladder leading down to what looked like fake grass. There were glittering torches lighting the way—not with fire, but with some sort of magical light that cast sparkles all over the walls and the see-through ceiling.

"Yay," Haran said with an excited grin. "We get to see more dinosaur bones."

Seven smiled. That was the brother she knew and loved. Never mind the fact that he was too weak to walk. She would just ignore that little detail and focus on the positive.

She lifted them all down, quite pleased with herself that she could carry something as big as Mappy when she flew. That little tidbit might come in handy some day. Mappy squealed the entire twelve seconds it took to make it to the ground, which was not fake grass, as Seven had first suspected, but some kind of magical grass that was soft and cushy. "Should we eat before we get started? I have no idea how long this tunnel is, but at the other end is something I'm supposed to battle, so eating now might be a good idea." The thought sent shivers up and down her spine. Nervous didn't even begin to sum up how she felt. How, exactly, was one supposed to feel as one was facing imminent death?

That was a very good question.

So she tried not to think about it. Or she obsessed about it, planning, going over everything she knew about Krakens—which wasn't much. Apparently they had an "in" with demons, because she'd been sending them after Seven every step of the way. Which meant she must also be friends with the seer, or she wouldn't know where Seven would *be*. They ate quickly and then started on their way. No point delaying the inevitable any longer than necessary. The fact that the point of Seven's entire journey waited at the end of the tunnel was not lost on her. It would have been easier if she'd just stumbled across Lady Kraken along the way. Less time to freak herself out.

"Hey," Haran said, interrupting her inner panic. "Get out of your own head."

Seven blinked at him and then couldn't help

but smile. He knew her too well. "Good idea. Talk to me, Haran."

He nodded. "Sure. But maybe we should clean out Mappy's ears so he can talk, too. He seems to enjoy that."

Seven slapped herself in the forehead. "Oh! I completely forgot! Poor Mappy!" She dug in her bag and grabbed a water bottle, checking three times to make sure it wasn't Haran's life-saving water, and used it to clean out Mappy's ears. He looked around in wonder as if he was just waking up in the tunnels instead of having walked himself there.

"Mappy hears you!" he exclaimed, clapping his hands enthusiastically. Seven was slightly amazed that he could clap and not drop Haran at the same time.

Haran looked less than thrilled about it, though, as he bounced around in Mappy's arms. "I will be so glad when I have enough energy to walk again. I feel like a giant baby," he grumbled.

"Nah. You have too much hair to be a giant baby." Seven ruffled his shaggy head, giggling as sand (from who-knew which leg of their journey) rained down on her. She ducked out of the way as Haran half-heartedly slapped at her.

"So," she said as they hurried down the tunnel. "We know that Lady Kraken is huge. We know that she has lots of arms—"

"Like an octopus. With a woman's head and upper body. Mythology loves animal bodies with people heads," Haran interrupted.

She nodded. "Okay. So, woman's head and upper body. Eight arms with suckers on them, I'm guessing?"

Mappy nodded. "Suckers. Latch on and suck out soul."

Seven pulled a face. "Well that sounds . . . unpleasant. What else do we know?"

"She has no special powers. She's just big. And she's slow." Haran waved his arms around like a miniature Kraken. Seven had never been so grateful for his obsession with mythology than she was now—and she'd had a lot of chances to be grateful for it on this trip. "Look! We're leaving the land and going under the water!" Haran crowed, forgetting the serious conversation they were in the middle of.

But it was true. They left dirt, dinosaur bones and worms behind and entered an underwater tunnel. The ceiling and walls were clear, but the floor was still covered in the grassy stuff. "Do you think we'll see a shark? Maybe a whale?" Haran asked, his eyes so wide Seven worried they might fall out of his head. She'd had that worry many times on this journey.

"I really, really hope not." Seven did not like fish. Or things that could eat her. Even with the tunnel around them, she wasn't particularly excited about seeing anything with big teeth. But she forgot all of that the further away from land they got. There were ship wreckages all around them. Big ships, ancient ships, little boats. All kinds of sea crafts. The tall mast of a boat that looked like it was straight out of a pirate movie lay right across the tunnel, the tattered remains of a flag still waving in the current. Most of them were covered in moss and creatures of the ocean, but some were newer and cleaner. And there were so many. "We must be in the Bermuda Triangle!" Seven gasped. Of course it made sense that the main tunnels to Atlantis would cross the Triangle.

She paused to press her face against the glass, studying everything with morbid curiosity. "This is so cool! If only the scientists of the world could walk for a few minutes in this tunnel. Think of all the answers they could find!"

She'd always been fascinated by mysteries. Lost ships, disappearing planes, unexplainable things. The Bermuda Triangle was the center of lots and lots of those occurrences. And she got to walk right through it. "Look at that plane! It's so old!" Her mind whirred. Amelia Earheart had maybe disappeared in the Bermuda Triangle. There were rumors. What if Seven saw her plane? She could barely contain her bouncing as she stared eagerly at all the wreckages.

"Do you think any of these have treasure?" Haran asked, looking just as excited as Seven felt. Mappy, on the other hand, looked bored. Almost like he might be sleep walking. That would be bad. If Mappy went to sleep and fell forward, Haran would get smooshed.

Seven squinted through the tunnel wall, trying to see into the deep hidden recesses of the ships. "That would be awesome," she murmured.

And then she screeched, clamping a hand over her mouth as the tunnel cracked under the weight of her cry. A shark, bigger than some of the ships they were watching, roared out of the darkness, big mouth wide with all its jagged rows of teeth. It smashed into the tunnel, but the strong walls thankfully held. Apparently, only Seven could cause irreparable damage.

It swung around for another try, clearly wanting to eat them all for lunch. It hit the glass four times before it gave up, its nose bloody and several teeth imbedded in the tunnel ceiling. Seven grabbed Mappy's hand and they took off, running as fast as her short legs would carry her. When she wasn't so busy watching the old ships and planes, she could see the sea life. Huge whales floated above them—bigger than her school bus. Their shark left them to rejoin a group of its friends—at least ten of them. Seven shivered as they caught an unfortunate school of fish and had *them* for lunch instead of her, Haran, and Mappy.

She would have loved to see dolphins, but it wasn't to be. She guessed they didn't come down as deep as the tunnels were, probably because of their need to breathe every so often. She was so busy watching for them, though, that she didn't realize they'd reached the end of the tunnel until it was almost too late.

CHAPTER SEVENTEEN: NICE TO MEET YOU, LADY KRAKEN

The long, sucker-covered arm smashed into the tunnel floor right in front of Seven's feet. "This gate is closed, impure. Go back where you belong."

Seven gasped and dove backward, chills racing up and down her spine at the woman's voice. It was deep and throaty and pure evil. She peered up from where she lay on the soft grass, trying to hide her trembling. The tunnel widened into a large room with the gate to Atlantis at the end of it. In front of the gate stood the thing that had been haunting Seven's nightmares since she'd been called on this journey.

Lady Kraken was beautiful. She had long

blond hair that swirled around her like she was in an ocean current. Two human arms crossed in annoyance over her chest and a gazillion tentacle-leg thingies wriggling around her. Deep sea-green eyes surrounded by impossibly long eyelashes glared at Seven. They didn't glow red like all the other demons Seven had fought. It took her several seconds to realize that Lady Kraken wasn't a demon. She was an Atlantian. Apparently she was on the bad guy's side.

"Mappy, take Haran out of her reach. If something happens to me—" she choked on her own fear and had to clear her throat several times before she could continue. "If something happens, have him drink the rest of the water and get him back to Ireland. Can you do that?"

"Seven, I can help!" Haran cried, his eyes wide and full of terror in his completely pale face. He'd been so brave this whole time.

Seven gave him a gentle smile. "Haran, every battle I've fought, you've been there to save the day. This time, I've got to do it on my own. You just be ready to drink that water as soon as the gate opens. Do you understand?"

Haran started to cry. Seven threw her arms around him, holding him tight and wishing so much that she never had to let him go. Mappy patted her on the head awkwardly, and Seven turned to face Lady Kraken.

She sucked in a deep breath and squared her shoulders, the way her dad had taught her when she had to face Death the first time and she'd been so scared. She felt him there now, whispering in her heart. And her mom, too. Both of them were with her. She wasn't alone.

"I'll give you one chance to move out of the way and let me open the gate."

Lady Kraken blinked at her, a slow grin spreading across her face. "A little banshee, are you? And you think you can beat me? You're so…" she eyed Seven up and down before her lip curled in disgust. "Small."

"I don't face you alone." Seven was shocked at the voice coming out of her mouth. There was no fear. It didn't shake like it should. She sounded brave. A few days ago, she hadn't even been able to stand up to the kids at school. Now here she was confronting a sea creature the size of her house with legs that could steal her soul, and she didn't sound scared a bit.

Lady Kraken glanced behind her. "The Mapinguari? He can do nothing against me."

Seven shook her head, walking forward, within reach of the tentacles. "No. Not him. He's just here to watch." She smirked at her own little joke, feeling strength flood her spine, bolstering her, lifting her until her feet weren't even on the ground. Apparently when the seer had told the sea creature where to send her demons, she hadn't told her much about what would happen once Seven made it here. Maybe they hadn't expected her to. Maybe the seer wasn't entirely on Lady Kraken's side. Seven didn't know and she didn't care. She was here, and she was strong enough. She had to be.

Lady Kraken moved slowly back and forth in front of the gate, her legs rolling underneath her. But Seven couldn't scream at this angle or she'd hit the tunnel and it would collapse. And flood. And they would all die.

Except Lady Kraken. Which was the opposite of what Seven was trying to do.

Lady Kraken looked completely baffled. "Then—who? You, confused little insignificant thing, are very alone."

"I'm never alone," Seven whispered. Just as two tentacles whapped down toward her, she grabbed the warmth and lit her eyes. The waves of fire exploded, shooting out toward the legs. She'd expected them to be cut off where her lasers swiped across them, but instead they both lit, burning despite the wet, slimy surface.

Lady Kraken screamed and beat them on the ground, forgetting completely about Seven as she tried to stop the flames. But Seven didn't forget. "Are you going to move so I can open the gate?"

Lady Kraken snarled as she whirled on her. "How did you do that? Banshees don't have any real power!"

"Hybrids do. I guess no one told you that. Now move. Please." Desperate times did not mean she couldn't still be polite.

Lady Kraken did not share her outlook. She screamed, which was ineffective and slightly ironic against a banshee. She swung three of her other, unwounded legs at Seven. Seven flew into the air, dodging two, but the third one hit her. She slammed backward into the wall and a shriek burst from her lungs. She'd forgotten. Forgotten the control Six had taught her.

Above, the tunnel cracked and water leaked in. Seven watched in horror as the crack spread further—toward Mappy and Haran. Mappy tried to shield them with his big hands as they were rained on, and then he tucked Haran under his arm and ran back the way they'd come.

Seven struggled to her feet, trying to forget about the crack. *Don't scream. Don't scream.*

The tunnel was filling with water. By the smug look on Lady Kraken's face, this pleased her. Already the water was up to Seven's ankles, pooling around her feet.

She looked up just in time to see more legs swinging toward her. She squeaked, clamping a hand over her mouth. The legs whacked her again, smashing her into the side of the tunnel and holding her there. This time, though, she kept her mouth shut. Instead, she closed her eyes, grabbed the heat, and let the flames free. Lady Kraken bellowed as the leg pinning Seven's stomach to the wall was scorched. The sea witch jerked her arms up, and water followed her hands, rising from the tunnel floor. With an angry roar, she flung the water at Seven, dousing her flames. So she did have powers. Seven supposed they'd both underestimated the other.

Awesome.

Seven gasped and choked and blinked, trying to clear the water from her eyes. Lady Kraken laughed, an evil, scary sound. Seven looked down the tunnel to where Haran fought to see her and Mappy tried desperately to keep him from looking.

Mappy thought she had lost.

Seven grunted, wriggling loose like she had with Akie the day he'd taken them from Ireland. She slid toward the floor as Lady Kraken's slimy scales struggled to hold her in place, finally catching her by the throat. The fatty blubber of one leg covered her mouth, slime oozing against her face.

She gagged and struggled to breathe as the leg cut off her air. She'd figured Lady Kraken would be hard, but Seven hadn't thought she'd get her butt kicked quite so bad. So this was how she would lose? By being strangled by an icky leg?

No. No, that is not how Seven planned on dying.

She bared her teeth, gagging a bit at the thought of what she was about to do. Then she bit down hard on the fleshy part closest to her. She tasted . . . yucky. Seven wasn't sure it was blood or if Lady Krakens had tar in their veins, but it was not a fun taste to have in her mouth.

However, it worked.

The leg jerked away from her as Lady Kraken screeched in pain, and Seven landed hard on the floor. Pain shot through her tailbone and her back as water soaked her clear up to her chest. This was getting serious. Struggling to her feet, she faced the evil sea thing again.

Too late.

Another leg hit her, but this time she didn't go flying. The suckers on the underside latched on, just like Mappy said they would, and as soon as one tentacle caught her, several others wrapped around her. She felt them pulling at her soul. Her soul, which seemed to be a creation of all the memories that made her who she was. Six, taking Haran's mother without even a glance at her tiny daughter because it was too painful for her. Her father, holding Seven close. Teaching her to walk. Taking her to school. Telling her to stay away from boys until she was thirty. Haran, stealing her toys, helping her practice cricket, making her laugh when she wanted to cry. And more recent, Death letting her take her brother even when he wasn't supposed to. Akie. Mappy. Six teaching her how to be a banshee. Her dad's voice in her head. And through it all, Haran being there every step of the way.

Seven refused to lose these memories. She'd worked too hard for them and they meant too much. She started to sing.

Her singing made Lady Kraken laugh. "Really? This is what you fight me with? Lullabies?"

Seven opened her eyes, smiling at her ghosts over Lady Kraken's shoulder. "No. *They* are what I fight you with."

Her ghosts surged forward, not waiting to be asked, attacking the legs that held Seven. Lady

Kraken screamed, lashing at the ghosts with her remaining tentacles, but they went uselessly through the spirits. The suckers released and Seven collapsed on the ground, breathing hard as she gathered her memories and tucked them away where they were safe. Then she stood up. "You shouldn't have done that."

Lady Kraken glared at her. "You think these can take me down? The lot of them can barely fight off one of my tentacles."

Seven didn't answer. She grabbed the warmth and lit her eyes. This time, the fire was fueled by her anger and both eyes were like lasers, slicing right through two of Lady Kraken's legs like she had hoped they would do the first time. A third one whacked Seven but didn't get a grip, only sent her flying sideways into the tunnel wall. Water soaked her as Lady Kraken threw the rising waves. Seven ducked and held her breath, waiting until the water ebbed away.

Before she could even see again, she struggled back to her feet and flew into the air, darting around Lady Kraken, slicing off legs that moved only half as fast as she could.

Tie them in knots, Sev.

Her dad's voice was such a welcome relief in her head that Seven almost sobbed. She darted through the legs, over and under, and wove them like she'd woven a mat with construction paper in school. The tentacles followed her, twisting in on themselves in their attempt to catch her. But they were too slow and Lady Kraken was too furious to realize what Seven was doing until it was too late.

Seven panted. She was exhausted already. And wet. And cold. Her eyes burned and staying in the air was difficult. But she hadn't come this far and survived this long to be defeated by her own weakness. So she ignored the pain and the tiredness and instead focused on her weaving.

Good girl, Seven.

It was her mom's voice this time.

The thought of being beaten by a tiny, dirty, insignificant girl must have been infuriating, and the anger made Lady Kraken move more slowly, just like Mappy had said.

Seven felt her confidence returning. She shot up toward the top of the tunnel, bouncing off like ping pong ball and ricocheting around, laser eyes flaming. Her ghosts cheered as the legs fell around them, burned and useless.

Three tentacles protected Lady Kraken's body. And she had way more than eight legs, like an octopus. But Seven was taking them down two at a time. They wouldn't last long. Even so, this wasn't killing her. And the legs Seven had attacked were slowly growing back. Seven needed to scream, to blow this sea witch right out of the way. But to do it, she had to be at the perfect angle or she'd hit the already-cracked tunnel and flood the entire city. Getting to that angle, though, was more than a little difficult with all the flying slimy tentacles. And she every so often caught glimpses of Mappy and Haran. The water was up to Mappy's waist now and Haran sat on his shoulders, watching with his fist against his mouth.

They were running out of time.

Seven dodged out of the way, twisting, riding on the air as the sea witch screamed and swung more raging legs at her. The first one missed, but the second one caught her, and again Seven was knocked into the tunnel wall. She slid slowly down, landing on her hands and knees. She tasted blood.

"Seven! I'm here!" she heard a voice, oddly familiar, and she struggled to see around the flames in her eyes to the source.

Cam. Cam had come.

"I told you, you wouldn't fight alone!" he yelled, leveling his trident at Lady Kraken as he fought to stay on his feet in the rapidly rising water.

Seven grinned.

Lady Kraken had thrown her exactly where she needed to be. She struggled to her feet, swaying dangerously. If Cam could just knock the sea witch back a few feet . . .

He seemed to read her mind. His trident exploded and hit Lady Kraken, knocking her back again and again as he dodged her remaining legs.

"Perfect," Seven whispered.

"Cam, get down!" Haran bellowed.

Seven opened her mouth. The scream that exploded from her throat was angrier, sharper, more terrifying than anything she'd ever done. It hit Lady Kraken like a giant wave. The sea witch gave one brief shriek before she was completely obliterated, raining fishy-smelling bits and pieces over them all. Seven ducked, holding her arms over her head as tentacle suckers pelted her, but without Lady Kraken's force behind them, they had no power. There was a roar and a crack and the sound of falling, splashing rock. Seven kept her head down and prayed Haran was doing the same.

CHAPTER EIGHTEEN:
HI DAD, CAN I KEEP HIM?

Seven raised her head. Haran and Mappy were splashing toward her. Cam was staring over her shoulder. Her ghosts surrounded her protectively, but there was nothing else to protect her from. "Haran! Are you okay?" she raced to meet them, half-swimming now.

Haran nodded. "Are you? You killed her, Seven! You killed the Kraken!"

Seven smiled, plucking bits of what looked like sushi out of Mappy's matted fur and Haran's floppy hair. "I'm okay. Battered and bruised, but I'm okay."

"Seven!" Cam yelled, wading toward them. "Use your hot eyes to seal the cracks!"

My hot eyes? Belatedly, Seven realized what he meant and looked up, willing the flames to her eyes. They burned the glass tunnel, melting it back together. The leaking water stopped, but she could see it bubbling already. Her fix was only temporary.

She turned to her ghosts. "You were amazing. As always. When all hope was lost, you came." She fought against the tears that fell from her eyes, healing them from the burns. "I could not have done this without you."

Grandmother Macfarland patted her cheek. "Of course you could have. We just helped things along a bit." The rest of them nodded in agreement before they raised one hand and faded away.

"Um, Seven?" Cam asked, his voice hesitant from behind them.

She turned, the grin dying on her face. The gate had collapsed. Instead of breaking it open, she'd broken it into a million giant boulders. Once it had been surrounded by ornate statues of mermaids, but now one was missing a face and another was missing a tail, and the entire entryway was completely blocked.

"What have I done?" she moaned as she stared at the disaster. The tunnel, too, was almost completely blocked. She'd covered everything with broken gate pieces.

"Well . . . you were supposed to open the gate, and you collapsed it. No offense, Seven, but I think that didn't go according to plan," Cam pointed out as if she somehow hadn't noticed.

Seven glared at him, turning in circles. "We'll rebuild it. No problem."

Haran pushed on a boulder the size of a small car. "I think . . . that isn't possible." Not only was the gate blocked by collapsed tunnel pieces, but the tunnel had huge chunks loose, too, and water poured around them. This was bad. So bad.

"I got this!"

Seven whirled around, hope nearly exploding her heart as Colin, the boy she'd met and fought with at the Pyramids, came sprinting up the tunnel, dodging falling pieces of rock as he hurdled debris.

"You . . . got this? Can you fix this?" Seven

asked. "I didn't have a choice. That thing was going to kill us all—I had to scream—"

Colin gave her a lopsided grin. "No worries. I can fix this. Just . . . stay out of my way. I mean that in the nicest way possible."

Seven held up her hands and backed off. "You got it." Colin disappeared behind the rubble, and Seven ran a hand through her wild hair. "I can't believe I did this. Stupid scream!"

Haran touched her arm. "Your stupid scream saved us all. Don't forget that."

"And it can save us again," Cam said, "Scream at the boulders, Seven."

She gaped at him, looking at the fallen gate, some pieces of which were as big as her house in Ireland. "You want me to scream. Again. Are we trying to collapse the whole city? Because I think that's what they're trying to save here, Cam."

Cam rolled his eyes. "Scream, banshee. Shatter the boulders. Open the broken gate."

Seven's mouth formed in a silent "*Oh*", and she slapped her hand to her forehead. "Right. I can do that. I can break it up and open a path and Colin can fix it!"

Cam raised an eyebrow and Haran grinned. "Go get it, banshee girl."

She closed her eyes, digging for her banshee roots way down deep in her soul. When she opened her mouth, Cam and Haran and Mappy all dove out of the way and she screamed, felt it shake the tunnel, heard Colin yell, and mentally apologized, and the boulders shattered into a thousand and one falling pebbles. She ducked, covering her head for the second time in ten minutes, as stones rained down on them. Cam held his shield above the four of them until the deluge stopped. Seven dropped her hands, peering through the dust.

The gate was open.

"That'll be easier to fix. Thanks!" Colin sounded much too enthusiastic for almost being caught in a collapsing tunnel.

"That's one tough kid," Haran said, watching as Colin ran off to fix the beams of the gate.

Seven ruffled his hair. "So are you, little brother." And then Seven remembered. Remembered the reason for her entire journey here. "Haran! Drink! Hurry!" Seven splashed down the tunnel to where their packs floated, caught on parts of fallen tunnel. She jerked the precious water bottle out of the bag and thrust it at Haran. He took it, almost shyly, and drank. In only two swallows, the color returned to his face, his cheeks turned a healthy pink and his brown eyes were bright again. He did a happy little dance around them, splashing in the water.

"I'm okay! I'm okay, Sev! Look!" he crowed, jumping into the air. Seven couldn't help it. She laughed and cried and danced with him.

He grinned and bounced on his toes.

She peered through the gate. Riots raged, and the beautiful mythical city of Atlantis wasn't faring so well. "They need help," she murmured.

People ran back and forth past the gate, too busy to see the crumbled remains Seven had left. She was so caught up watching them that she completely missed Death until he was nearly on top of her. "Death! You said—" she squeaked.

Haran ran behind her in alarm. Cam and Mappy looked around them frantically, but of course they couldn't see him. Only Seven could see the red glowing eyes and long black robes as he floated closer. "I'm not here for your brother, little banshee." He raised a long finger and pointed at a man who strode by, surrounded by several soldiers.

"Hey! Hey!" Seven yelled, stumbling closer to the man. He glanced over his shoulder and glared at her before he started to turn away. "Death—Death follows you. You need—"

He cut her off with an annoyed wave of his hand. "Death follows us all, little girl." He stormed away and Seven started to follow him, to warn him, to give him a chance to say goodbye to those he loved, maybe, but Cam stopped her.

"That's Phoibos, Seven. Let him go."

Seven's eyes widened as she watched Death turn to go. That was the mighty bad guy who'd sent all the demons to stop her? That was the guy trying to purge all the hybrids in Atlantis?

Cam cleared his throat, pulling her away from the gate to the relative quiet of the tunnel. "Seven, I thought maybe you'd like to talk to your father. I tagged you on SplashSpace and asked if anyone could get in touch with him." Cam held out a tablet. It was blue and shiny, more magic-y looking than Seven's, but she recognized the Splashpace page right away.

She took the tablet, raising hope-filled, questioning eyes to him. "My dad is on here—?"

"On your page, actually. Hi Sev."

Seven sobbed as she jerked her eyes back to the screen and Haran leaped over her shoulder so he could see, too. "Dad?" they both yelled.

Her dad's face bloomed on the screen and he smiled, even as tears stained his cheeks. "Hi guys. Seven, you were supposed to check in occasionally. You're grounded for life."

Seven laughed around a sob. "I'm okay with that. I don't ever want to leave the house again."

"Are you okay, then? I see Haran—did you escape Death?" The hope in his voice would have shattered Seven's heart a few minutes ago. But now Haran was here, all better, with no more Death chasing him.

"Yes! Haran is just fine! He's all better! Haran, show him how good you look!"

Haran rolled his eyes, but he took the tablet from her. "Hi Dad. How's it going?" His finger, seemingly without him even noticing, traced the outline of their dad's face on the screen as his tears splashed around it.

Their dad chuckled, but Seven could tell he was crying, too. "I'm good, Haran. I have a friend of yours here. He said you gave him permission to live with us."

"Akie! He made it?" Seven squealed.

Her dad's eyes crinkled. "Yes. Are you guys okay? Really okay? Have you finished your quest yet?"

Seven nodded. "Yeah, Dad. We're okay. And we're done. We'll start home soon. And we're bringing home a new friend, too. We wouldn't have made it without him."

Cam's eyes widened. "You don't—you don't mean me, do you?"

Seven giggled. "No. Mappy. Mappy is coming home with us."

Her dad heaved an exaggerated sigh and nodded. "I suppose. Just hurry home, okay? I've missed you guys."

Seven had so much to tell him. So much to explain, so many things that had changed. She longed to tell him about Six, but now wasn't the time. Atlantis was facing war—she could still hear the rioting behind her. So instead, she forced a bright smile and nodded. "We'll be home soon, Dad. I promise." She kissed her fingers and laid them against the screen. Haran did the same.

"I love you guys," their dad said, also touching his fingers to the screen.

"Love you too, Dad."

Seven handed the tablet back to Cam. "Thank you. Thank you so much for that."

Cam smiled. "No problem. So . . . now what?"

Seven glanced over her shoulder at the raging battle. "I think I'm almost done, but not quite. Haran, what do you think?"

Haran grinned, his eyes bright. "I think we came too far not to go check things out inside."

Seven nodded her agreement and Haran darted toward the now-open gate. "Haran, wait—" she called. He paused and looked over his shoulder. "You're the best little brother ever."

He grinned and ran back, throwing his arms around her neck. "I love you, too, Sev. Now let's go see who else we can beat up today!"

THE GATES OF ATLANTIS

BANSHEE AT THE GATE
BY: WENDY KNIGHT

GUARDIANS OF THE GATES
BY: LAURA D. BASTIAN

SECRETS OF THE MINE
BY: JULI CALDWELL

MAGICIANS OF THE DEEP
BY: JACLYN WEIST

MADNESS BEHIND THE THRONE
BY: J.R. SIMMONS

BATTLE FOR ACROPOLIS
BY: MIKEY BROOKS

ABOUT THE AUTHOR

Wendy Knight is the bestselling author of the young adult series *Fate on Fire* and *Riders of Paradesos*. She was born and raised in Utah by a wonderful family who spoiled her rotten because she was the baby. Now she spends her time driving her husband crazy with her many eccentricities (no water after five, terror when faced with a live phone call, no touching the knives…you get the idea). She also enjoys chasing her three adorable kids, playing tennis, watching football, reading, and hiking. Camping is also big—her family is slowly working toward a goal of seeing all the National Parks in the U.S. You can usually find her with at least one Pepsi nearby, wearing ridiculously high heels for whatever the occasion. And if everything works out just right, she will also be writing.

Follow Wendy Knight on all her social media sites:
Blog: www.wendyknightauthor.blogspot.com
Facebook: www.facebook.com/AuthorWendyKnight
Twitter: https://twitter.com/wjk8099
Instagram: http://instagram.com/wendyjo99
Wattpad: http://wattpad.com/WendyKnight

OTHER BOOKS BY WENDY KNIGHT

<u>THE FATE ON FIRE SERIES</u>

FEUDLINGS

FEUDLINGS IN FLAMES

FEUDLINGS IN SIGHT

FEUDLINGS IN SMOKE

THE SPARK OF A FEUDLING

<u>THE RIDERS OF PARADESOS SERIES</u>

WARRIOR BEAUTIFUL

WARRIOR EVERLASTING

<u>COMING SOON</u>

WARRIOR INNOCENT
(RIDERS OF PARADESOS BOOK 3)

SHATTERED ASSASSIN

ROCKER BOY

If you enjoyed this book
please leave a review at:

AMAZON.COM

BARNESANDNOBLE.COM

KOBO.COM

GOODREADS.COM

For signed copies or more information on
other books by Wendy Knight visit:

www.GatesofAtlantis.com

Keep reading for a sneak peek at:

THE GATES OF ATLANTIS:
GUARDIANS OF THE GATES

By LAURA D. BASTIAN

CHAPTER ONE:
NEVER TICK OFF A GIRL

Atlantis was a prison.

Exander stood in front of the barrier leading to the ocean and took a deep breath. He didn't actually need the oxygen since his lungs would filter the water just fine in his Mer form, but it always helped him with the temperature change. He took hold of the silver wrap around his waist, ready to remove it as soon as he left the city of Atlantis, and then dove head first into the clean, cool water.

The second the water hit his lower body, his legs transformed into fins—silver with black stripes shooting down from his hips to the tips of his tail. He could leave the city itself, but what good was the ability to be part Merman, part human if he never got to go to the world above?

He tucked the wrap into his bag and pushed the strap until the bag rested on his back. Exander swam to the ocean floor in search of something to eat. His parents were at another meeting and didn't bother to make any dinner. He wasn't quick enough to catch fish in the schools. Most times they saw him coming and flitted off in a million directions leaving him flustered and hungry.

A crab, sea urchin, or bottom dweller would be a sure bet. Not as tasty to eat raw, but still good enough for a snack. After scoring his meal, he headed toward the gate his brother Lyle helped guard. His shift would be over soon and they could return home together. By then his parents might have started to care where he was.

Two guardians flanked the gate leading from the bottom of the ocean to a place in the world above. Someone smaller guarded the side Lyle's friend Sloan usually guarded. Sloan's younger sister, Talia, floated in the water next to the gate holding his trident. Her iridescent blue fins caught the light filtering from the glowing orb above the gate and Exander couldn't help being relieved his own fins were more muted. Nothing fancy like hers. He didn't need more reasons for people to tease him. He got enough of that in his human form. Lyle assured him he'd had long skinny legs and gangly arms at thirteen as well. Exander couldn't wait until his body morphed into the bulging biceps and broad chest his brother had.

"What're you doing, Talia?" Exander asked as he got closer. "Only trained guards are allowed tridents." She was still five years away from being old enough to be a guardian of the gate.

"What'cha gonna do?" she asked. "Tell?"

Exander bristled at the words and shook his head. Exander turned to Lyle. "Where's Sloan?"

"He got sick. Talia got permission from the general to fill in for him since the shift is almost over." He smiled at her.

"Why didn't you say so?" Exander turned to Talia.

"You didn't ask."

Exander frowned. Talia had changed these last couple of months. They used to get along well. Now she was always moody and took everything he said wrong. She was still mad at him for teasing her about Cam, an Atlantian guard.

Talia rolled her grey-blue eyes and Exander turned back to Lyle for help. Lyle shrugged and swam a few meters away, leaving him to face Talia alone. Maybe Lyle was smart enough to know when to give them a minute. Exander only wished he could return things to the way they used to be.

"I'm sorry, Talia. I shouldn't have jumped to conclusions." He bowed his head, not sure what else to say. He looked up. Talia floated there with her mouth open.

"Uh, thanks," Talia finally managed to say. Exander examined the gate as an excuse to not make eye contact with her. Something good had happened and he didn't want to risk messing it up by speaking.

The gate was shaped like a pyramid. Made of solid gold and ten feet high from the bottom to the tip. The light from the orb on top illuminated the symbols and words on the gateway. Some were recognizable to him, but others were in a completely foreign language. The doorway went up about seven feet and appeared to be water from the side, but straight on a shimmer from some other source was visible. He wondered if the entrance to the gate in the upper world was in the direct sunlight.

The back of the gate had no opening, just solid gold. He'd never traveled through a gate, but knew they opened up into a passageway between the surface and the bottom of the ocean. Eight gates like this one surrounded Atlantis, each about a mile from the city's barrier. Though he understood the basic principal of how the gates worked, it was such an ancient magic that no one seemed to know the details.

Lyle offered Exander his trident. "Can you stay here a second while I go talk to a man about a seahorse?"

Exander nodded and took up Lyle's position.

"What do you think you're doing?" Talia gasped in mock surprise. "Don't you know only official guards are allowed tridents?"

Exander turned to her. "I said I was sorry."

Talia didn't respond, just turned her back to

the gate. Exander watched her for a moment while the current moved her long brown hair slightly. Usually she had it pulled back tight in a braid so it didn't tangle, but he liked the way it flowed easily when she undid it in the water.

"How were your classes?" Exander asked.

"Good."

"Mine were good too. Thanks for asking," Exander said.

"Your classes are always good. I didn't think I had to ask."

"No, they're not," Exander argued.

"Of course they are. You get perfect scores on all tests without studying. You don't have any issues with any of the teachers and you're basically the poster boy for education."

"You're mad at me because I do well in school?"

"I'm not mad at you." Talia crossed her arms over her chest.

"Yes, you are. You've been mad at me for months now and I can't figure out why."

Talia opened her mouth, shut it, opened it again, then frowned. She took a slow breath.

"Everything is perfect for you."

Exander rolled his eyes. "What world are you living in?"

Her gaze turned to Atlantis and she raised one eyebrow at him. He knew she loved the city and everything the Mer stood for as they helped protect it. Exander wished he could get away and see the rest of the world. Talia never cared what was up there, even called him stupid for thinking of being an explorer. She wanted to be a guardian of the gates so bad he wasn't surprised she got permission to stand in for her brother.

Exander looked at the gate again. "Where does this gate lead to on the surface?"

"It's in the country of Algeria in Africa. It's by some huge monolith near a cliff."

"Is it sunny there?" Exander asked.

"I guess. I don't know. Why?"

Exander motioned for Talia to join him in front of the gate. "Do you see the reflection of light on the surface of the doorway?"

Talia nodded.

"Wouldn't that be from sunlight?"

"Possible, but all of the gates I've seen have

this same reflection. And not all of the gates would be out in the light. Plus, they are like this all the time, and the sun isn't shining in those locations constantly."

Exander nodded. So his theory didn't pan out, but the light had to reflect off something. He saw this same design in places where the sunlight penetrated deep enough. And the time he took a fast trip to the surface of the Atlantic Ocean on a dare from Lyle.

"How many other gates have you visited?" Exander asked.

Talia shrugged. "All of the ones out in the water. I haven't been able to sneak into the one in the palace area. Or the one near the Collective in the center of Acropolis. They're guarded much more strictly since anyone can come through."

Exander nodded. It was impressive the Mer were the only ones trusted enough to guard the gates and to assist any visitors. If they didn't have a physical connection with a Mer they couldn't enter the barrier. And if they couldn't breathe underwater they would die pretty quick. The Mer escorting the visitor would breathe into their mouth and give them temporary magic, allowing their lungs the ability to filter the water.

"And all the ones out in the water have this same light display?" Exander asked.

"Yup."

"Have you ever been inside one of the gates?"

"No." Talia frowned, her forehead wrinkling like she was disgusted with the idea. "There is no way you'd get me to go up to the surface."

"It sounds fascinating to me."

"Haven't you heard what it's like there now?" Talia asked. "If we're lucky a plague will wipe out those nasty human creatures and we could return Atlantis to the surface. Once things were purged enough for our magic to be unfettered."

"Where did you get that ridiculous idea from?" Exander asked.

"It's not ridiculous," Talia said. "The Ruling Council says the surface dwellers are ruining things. Their pollution makes the magic do weird things. That's why most Mer have to use the tridents to focus the magic."

"That's not true." Exander held Lyle's trident

up. "They have always been used even before any pollution came to the ocean. Only General Triton could use magic without the trident. Every other Mer in history has used them."

"I can work some magic without a trident," Talia said, her face full of pride.

Exander couldn't help wanting to egg her on. "No, you can't."

Talia's scales shimmered in the light coming off the front of the gate. "I can too. I'll prove it."

"What are you going to do, try to freeze me?"

"Shut up. I only did that once." Talia scowled, but the sparkle in her eyes proved she wasn't angry anymore.

"And poorly too. You only got half of me frozen." He loved teasing her and it felt good that she was responding to his jabs.

"I meant to do that. Didn't want you to suffocate. Though why I cared is a mystery to me."

Exander looked her up and down. "What would you do with magic? Give me Sloan's trident and show me."

"I'm not giving you both tridents."

Exander grinned. "Because you don't have any magic without it."

"I do too."

"Liar."

Talia's pale face darkened and Exander wondered if he took the teasing too far. And just when he thought maybe they were friends again. Exander raised his hand to try to offer his apology, but Talia tossed the trident into the sand next to the gate and stretched her arms out to the side.

Exander could feel a charge in the water near him and he realized too late she told the truth. Talia had magic on her own and didn't need the trident to direct it. She pulled energy from the water and it swirled around in small flurries near her palms. She moved her arms toward each other and the balls of magic joined together, tripling in size. The water around Talia rippled and the light got brighter and brighter. Talia's face scrunched up in panic as the ball got larger still.

"Oh no! I can't hold it." The energy blast out in a powerful concussion throwing the two of them back.

Talia slammed into the gate and the magic flowing around her activated the opening. Exander watched in horror as her upper body disappeared into the doorway. He had only been thrown back about a yard so he kicked toward her.

He yanked on Talia's fin and pulled her out. She was still full of energy making the gate fizz and spark. Blasts of light shot out into the dark water. Exander threw himself against the gate, trying to figure out how to shut it off. He shoved the trident against the edge, hoping to absorb some of the excess energy. Pain shot through his arm and the trident burned like fire. A whirlpool coming from the open gate churned around him. He struggled to swim away from it, but it pulled harder than he could fight.

Exander released the trident when he found himself sucked into the gate. He hit the floor hard, stunned he had transformed into a boy when he touched the air. He looked up to see the gate was closed from the water.

Exander jumped up and pounded on the doorway. It was different from the inside. A light with no visible source illuminated an enormous white, barren tunnel with a door made from ancient wood. He ran his hand across it, feeling for any indication of a seam or crack. He felt nothing along the outer edge.

How did people who came through the gates get out? The guardians must know some way to open it. He pounded and kicked. He touched the scorched trident to the door and still nothing. Exander couldn't feel any of the latent magical power of the trident he felt earlier. Had it been destroyed when it connected to the magic of the gate, or was there no magical power access in the tunnel?

Exander had to calm down. He pulled his bag from behind his back and took out his wrap. He tied it around his waist and pulled out his school tablet to send Talia a message. He tried to power it on, but it didn't work.

Exander closed his eyes. If he focused hard enough, he'd be able to remember everything he had read about how the gates worked.

18479147R00167

Made in the USA
San Bernardino, CA
15 January 2015